PENGUIN BOOKS
1993

WAYS AND MEANS

HENRY CECIL

D1150761

WAYS AND MEANS

HENRY CECIL

PENGUIN BOOKS
IN ASSOCIATION WITH
MICHAEL JOSEPH

Penguin Books Ltd, Harmondsworth, Middlesex
AUSTRALIA : Penguin Books Pty Ltd, 762 Whitehorse Road,
Mitcham, Victoria

—

First published by Chapman & Hall 1952
Published by Michael Joseph 1960
Published in Penguin Books 1963

—

Copyright © Henry Cecil, 1952

—

Made and printed in Great Britain
by Cox and Wyman Ltd,
London, Reading, and Fakenham
Set in Monotype Baskerville

CONTENTS

Chapter 1

THE DISAGREEABLE MAN

It was a prosperous little community which lived round Tapworth Magna. They had cars and horses and quite enough capital to keep them going for the moment. Their houses were comfortable and full of good things, pictures, furniture, silver, wine, and even some domestic servants. There was hunting and shooting, tennis and cricket, the Stock Exchange and farming to keep them occupied. The younger men were inclined to be athletic, the younger women were attractive and looked well on and off horses. Both men and women talked quite a lot about themselves and each other but there were additional indoor amusements, such as bridge and canasta. Nearly all the men played at some time or other for the village cricket team, all the women went to the village institute. The congregation at church was never normally less than ten. After church one of the ten took some of the others home for drinks, so that there was always something to look forward to, even if the sermon was a bit long. It usually was. The Reverend Maitland Temperley was a good man and a good Vicar but he liked the sound of his own voice. On one rare occasion, when most of the local inhabitants, who normally attended church, were away or ill and the weather was very bad, the congregation consisted of the verger, three choirboys, the gardener from Tapworth Lodge (who sang in the choir), Mrs Thwaites, who kept the village store and Post Office (and was slightly deaf), and Simon Copplestone, who was very old and a little queer in the head.

None the less the Vicar delivered a full-length sermon and it took half an hour. Simon Copplestone and Mrs Thwaites had to be woken up at the end of the service. But the Vicar did not mind in the least. He knew that one person was listening all the time and enjoying the flow of words – himself. Apart from this failing, he was an admirable country parson and none the worse for being in possession of a substantial private income. He worked just as hard as though his living depended on it, and everyone liked and respected him.

One of the residents nearest to his church was a former High Sheriff of the county, Major-General Sir Bragge Purbrick. He was a good-natured man and friendly to most human beings and some animals. He had retired from the Army at the end of the war but had remained a leader of men. His nearest neighbour was a widow, Isabel Stroud. She was a selfish and determined woman of between forty and fifty, but she was intelligent, bright and gay and looked only about thirty-five. Her behaviour was always apparently beyond reproach and no breath of scandal had ever circulated about her. Nevertheless, an acute observer might have detected from time to time a look on her face which suggested that she kept, or would have liked to keep, something rather nice in the woodshed. Near her lived the local County Court judge, His Honour Judge George Strachan. He was a competent judge, though not really outstanding, and his chief claim to fame in the neighbourhood was his knowledge of Gilbert and Sullivan. In the days of Henry Lytton and Leo Sheffield he had been to performances on innumerable occasions and it was often his very great pleasure to sing songs from the operas in their manner. His memory for Gilbert's works was prodigious and he seldom missed an opportunity to quote. Here he was aided by Dr Sainsbury, who, although not so well up in the operas as the judge, was a good second. One of their regular turns together was the duet from the *Yeomen of the Guard*, 'Hereupon we're both agreed'. They always obliged with this when they were asked and sometimes when they were not. About half a mile from Dr Sainsbury lived Mr and Mrs Gaspard, two of the most popular people in the neighbourhood, and probably the most wealthy. They had a large estate and a large family. The youngest boy was once asked what he wanted to be when he grew up – a soldier like his eldest brother, a barrister like the next, a politician like the third, or what? 'I think I'd prefer just to muck about like Dad,' he replied.

There were others, too, who fitted into the scheme of things and a happy scheme it was. Neither two wars nor the Welfare State, neither bulk buying nor planned economy, neither nationalization nor surtax had uprooted the people round Tapworth Magna. The village life, too, went on in much the same way as in the past. True, a few ugly houses were put up by the Poppleton Council (Poppleton was the nearest town – some five miles away), but although this project caused some alarm and despondency and a good deal of plain speaking, the houses duly went up and life duly went on.

To Tapworth Magna there came one day two strangers. They took a small house which had been empty ever since its owner had died some few months before. It was said that they paid some £3,000 for it, rather more than it was worth. Basil Merridew was the elder and Nicholas Drewe the younger. If you had seen them at the time they came to Tapworth Magna you would have said that there were about fifteen years between them. You might also have summed up their respective characters by saying that Nicholas Drewe was a man whose instinctive reaction, on being bumped by some clumsy person in the street, was to say: 'I'm awfully sorry,' but that the reaction of Basil Merridew when, owing to his own carelessness, he collided with someone, was at least to glare and probably to add: 'Why the devil don't you look where you are going?'

Soon after they had taken possession of their house the Vicar called. The door was opened by Nicholas.

'I thought I'd just look around to see how you were settling in. I'm the vicar, you know.'

'How very kind of you,' said Nicholas. 'Do please come in. I'm afraid my uncle isn't at home at the moment, but, if you can spare a few moments, perhaps he will be back before you go.'

They went into the sitting-room and soon were chatting in a most friendly manner. This was not surprising. Nicholas was a man who could get on with everyone, and he had a knack of keeping the conversation to matters which interested the other party instead of keeping to his own pet subjects, however boring they might be to the listener. Naturally enough, in the circumstances, the talk soon came round to the church. The Vicar was delighted to find that Nicholas was not only a regular churchgoer but took a great interest in church architecture.

'The last incumbent – Wellsby Meeson-Smith,' said the Vicar, 'used to say that a fragment of a brass we have here is earlier than the one at Stoke D'Abernon.'

'Indeed,' said Nicholas. 'I did notice a fragment, but I'm surprised to hear you say that. It seemed to me to be fourteenth century. Perhaps I didn't see the one to which you're referring.'

'Oh yes, I think you did,' replied the Vicar. 'I entirely agree with you, but old Meeson-Smith had a bee in his bonnet about it. I'm sure he was quite wrong.'

'Meeson-Smith,' said Nicholas reflectively. 'I seem to remember the name somehow. Now in what connexion, I wonder?'

'Oh, dear,' said the Vicar. 'We shall never live it down, I'm afraid. Not that I'm criticizing him at all. He was a very good chap and entitled to his own amusements. You're thinking of the horse-racing case.'

'Oh – yes, of course. The parson who could pick winners and never backed them.'

'That was ten years ago,' said the Vicar, 'but I still get inquiries for him sometimes.'

'I'm not a betting man myself,' said Nicholas.

They went on talking for half an hour or so, and at last the Vicar had to leave, before Basil returned.

'I'm so sorry. I hope to see your uncle very soon.'

'If you would forgive a rather scratch meal, perhaps you would dine with us one day next week?' said Nicholas.

'How very kind of you, I should love it.'

So they fixed a day and the Vicar departed, very pleased with his visit.

It was not long before Nicholas and Basil had other callers. The Vicar had quickly circulated the news that one at least of the new arrivals was charming. His verdict was agreed to unanimously. Nicholas was a real acquisition. He was a good cricketer, a reasonable shot, very modest about such of his achievements as were dragged out of him, and very pleased to deliver a lecture to the Women's Institute on the Middle East, where he had served during the 1939–45 War. He easily retained this popularity. The opinion about Basil was different. People found him inclined to be taciturn and even boorish, but Nicholas was such an asset to the community that they accepted the older man with as good a grace as possible, and soon all the houses in the neighbourhood were open to them both. There was only one person who seemed to find more pleasure in Basil's company than in that of Nicholas – Mrs Stroud. She had hesitated a little, rather like a hawk poised in mid-air, and then, surprisingly enough, she had struck and struck hard at Basil. The reason for this must partly have been that she was the one person in whose company Basil seemed to relax and be pleasant and cheerful. He even paid her attractive compliments. On the other hand, although Nicholas was nice to everyone, Mrs Stroud seemed to detect, to her annoyance and surprise, a polite lack of interest in her on his part. So she turned to the elder. After all, too, she was much nearer his age and she would have preferred to be younger than her husband. Basil responded quickly and soon they were always in and out of each other's houses.

After about two months Basil's behaviour, never good, began to deteriorate markedly, except towards Mrs Stroud. To her he was always the soul of courtesy, and in her presence he was talkative, cheerful, and even gay. Towards others, however, he began not simply to be boorish, but even to be rude. But for Nicholas, who remained as popular as ever and who always tried to bring his uncle into everything, he would not have been tolerated. One day the Vicar called to see Nicholas and was disappointed to find only Basil in. With hardly a word of greeting, Basil led him into the sitting-room.

'Well,' he said, 'what have you come for? Want me to write your sermon? Why bother? No one listens.'

'Really, Mr Merridew, it is quite unnecessary to be so offensive.'

'Well, what *have* you come for? I don't remember inviting you.'

'In point of fact, I've come to see your nephew.'

'Well, can you see him?'

'Is he in, please?'

'He is not.'

'Then I don't think I'll wait.'

'I don't remember suggesting that you should.'

'Really, Mr Merridew, your behaviour is intolerable. Good afternoon.'

'Shut the door quietly after you, please.' The Vicar was a mild-mannered man and slow of temper, but, if Basil had not made reference to the door, he probably would have slammed it.

Basil did not behave in this way only to people like the Vicar. About three or four months after they had arrived he and Nicholas made a number of bulky purchases at Poppleton and brought them back in a hired car. The driver was extremely helpful and carried most of them into the house. It took him about five minutes and it was a very hot day.

'How much is that?' said Basil.

'The fare is seven-and-six.' Basil handed him seven-and-six. The driver looked at it and, thinking there must be some mistake, said:

'I said the *fare* was seven-and-six, sir.'

'Well, isn't that what I've given you?' said Basil and walked into the house. The driver was so taken by surprise that he could not at first think of any particular word to use (he had never driven a taxi in London), but, before he had made up his mind on the subject, Nicholas came out to him.

'Thank you very much,' he said and gave him five shillings. The driver was glad he had been so slow in the uptake.

After another couple of months of this sort of behaviour, people became unable to tolerate Basil even for Nicholas's sake. One or two of them were frank about it.

'I'm terribly sorry, old boy,' said Dr Sainsbury to Nicholas one day, 'but I simply can't ask your uncle. If I do, no one else will come. That goes for Barbara Newton too.'

She was one of the prettiest girls in the neighbourhood, and Nicholas had suggested to the doctor that he might include her in the party.

'I quite understand,' said Nicholas. 'I'll try to explain to you one day. It's a great shame, but I suppose it can't be helped.'

On another occasion the Vicar said to him:

'Nicholas, I don't mind saying that I have never met a comparatively young man such as you who combines so many of the virtues. I like you tremendously. All of us do.'

'You're much too generous.'

'But,' went on the Vicar, ' – and I feel I must speak plainly – I wish I could say the same for your uncle.'

'So do I,' said Nicholas. 'It's very difficult. Perhaps I'll tell you about it one day.'

He was to do so sooner than the Vicar expected.

On the Saturday following this conversation the village team was playing a neighbouring club at cricket on the village ground – or on what had been left of it after the Poppleton Council had had its way with the new houses. Basil was playing. It was pretty well the only social activity from which he had not yet been excluded. He was quite a good bat and a good slow bowler on a soft wicket. The other side batted first and Tapworth Magna went in after tea. Basil went in to bat at the fall of the third wicket. Nicholas was umpiring at the bowler's end. The first ball struck one of Basil's pads. There was a confident appeal. Nicholas signalled 'out'. Basil remained at the wicket. Nicholas signalled 'out' again. Basil signalled something back at him. A feeling of embarrassment swept across the field, involving players and spectators alike. 'Out,' said Nicholas, keeping his hand up.

Basil's reply was short but unprintable. 'I said "out", ' said Nicholas.

Basil's reply was very slightly longer but still unprintable. He remained at the wicket. General Purbrick, captain of the home team, started to get out of his deck-chair. Something had to be done and he, as captain, had to do it.

This is what actually went on in the General's mind, though it only took a few seconds:

Object. Is my object to get Merridew back to the pavilion (or its equivalent) with as little fuss and bother as possible or to finish with that bounder once and for all whatever happens? [Regretfully, he decided it must be the former.]

Considerations affecting the attainment of the object. Merridew has been given 'out'. Therefore he is 'out'. He is, however, staying in. Poor Nicholas is looking very unhappy. The longer Merridew stays there the worse it will be. What will the other side think of us? We could go out and drag him in, but that would be most undignified and might lead to a brawl.

Courses open to me. I can shout, 'come along, Merridew,' or words to that effect. I can walk out to him and tell him to leave the wicket. I can send someone who can get to him faster than I can to give him the message. If necessary, everyone will have to leave the field.

Courses open to Merridew. He can stay where he is. He can do what I tell him.

Plan. I shall go out to him myself and tell him to come in. If he refuses, I shall invite the captain of the other side to take his men off the field.

Meanwhile Nicholas remained almost motionless with his hand in the air. Basil remained at the wicket. Everyone else on the field stood as though his photograph were being taken. It was like a 'still' from a motion picture or a tableau, broken only by the slow movement of the General across the grass. At last he reached the wicket where Basil was and the silence was broken.

'Come along now, Merridew, you're out. Come on, man. Quick march.'

'You're not commanding your rotten platoon now,' said Basil.

For a moment the General looked as though he might collapse. His military training prevented him from even thinking of striking Basil, and yet his natural desire to do so was strong. The consequent tug-of-war inside him was a considerable strain. However, after a few seconds, he re-gained control of himself.

'If you do not leave the wicket immediately, everyone else will leave the field,' he said with dignity.

'Oh, all right,' said Basil, 'have it your own way. And as

for you,' he shouted to Nicholas, 'I'll see you when we get home.'

'Very well, Uncle,' said Nicholas meekly. Basil hurried from the pitch, followed more slowly by the General. As he neared the spectators they remained as tense as those in the field had been while the General had been walking to the wicket. He went past the spectators straight to the scorer, took the score book from in front of him, ripped the sheets out and tore them into small pieces. He then removed his pads, flung them to the ground and left the cricket field. It was quite a minute or two before people could start talking again.

'Come on,' said the General. 'Next man in.'

Mrs Stroud was not at the match. When news of the scene was reported to her all she said was: 'It's too bad, just because no one likes the man. I don't believe half of it.'

Five minutes later she got in her car and drove over to Basil's house. She found him in his shirt-sleeves gardening.

'I hope you don't mind my coming over,' she began.

'Come in, my dear,' he said. 'It's good to see you. What about a drink?'

And they had several.

That night Nicholas, carrying a small suitcase, arrived at the Vicarage. The Vicar opened the door and at once saw the suitcase and Nicholas's forlorn appearance.

'I think I know what you're going to say,' he said gently. 'The answer is: yes, of course. Stay here, my dear boy, as long as you like.'

For a moment Nicholas looked as though he were going to cry. Then he took the Vicar by the hand.

'I can only say "Thank you",' he said.

'It's nothing,' said the Vicar. 'It will be company for me and I shall be delighted. Now don't bother to explain anything. Come along and I'll show you your room. Mary,' and he called for the housekeeper.

It is hardly necessary to say that from that moment Basil was completely ostracized, except by Nicholas, who went across to see him from time to time, and by Mrs Stroud. Nicholas explained to the Vicar that Basil was his mother's brother, that he had always been a difficult person and that only she really understood and could manage him.

'Shortly before she died,' he told the Vicar, 'she asked me to promise to look after him. What could I say but yes? Of course, if he gets married that'll be different, and I'm bound to say – I don't know if you think it's wrong of me – I've some hopes of Mrs Stroud.'

'Well,' said the Vicar after a little reflection, 'I think she's quite capable of looking after herself. If she decides to marry your uncle, she'll know what she's about. I'm by no means sure that your uncle will, though. She's a very good woman, Mrs Stroud, no doubt, but, if ever anyone had determination, she has it. No – on the whole – if it comes off it may be for everyone's benefit – certainly for yours, my dear boy. You're very good to him. You must have had a very difficult time.'

'Oh – well, you know,' said Nicholas, 'I've managed.'

After this, life went on much as usual, though from time to time reference was made to the cricket match when there was a shortage of other things to talk about. Nicholas became part of the life round Tapworth Magna, and no one but he and Mrs Stroud spoke to Basil.

One day Mrs Thwaites called on the Vicar.

'I'm very sorry to trouble you, sir,' she said.

'That's quite all right, Mrs Thwaites. What can I do for you? Sit down.'

'I'm very worried, sir.'

'Well, tell me all about it. Take your time; there's no hurry,' and the Vicar looked at his watch.

'It's about that Mr Merridew, sir,' began Mrs Thwaites.

'Oh – has he been troubling you in some way?'

The Vicar was a devout and kindly man and a good Christian, but he had to repress a very definite feeling in him which seemed to say: 'Let's hope he has. Then we'll have a chance to get rid of him.' Side by side with this feeling was curiosity as to how Basil could have been troubling Mrs Thwaites. She was a highly respectable widow and, what was perhaps even more important, elderly and quite unattractive. Attributing everything that was bad to Basil – as the Vicar might have been prepared to do – he could not credit (or debit) him with designs against Mrs Thwaites.

'It's his bill, sir. He owes me over £30 and I can't get him to pay. I know I oughtn't to mention it, sir, but I'm so worried. I've got the rent to find and the shop doesn't give me more than a living. Everyone pays me except him, and I'm sure I don't –' But Mrs Thwaites could say no more and started to sob.

'There, there,' said the Vicar. 'You were quite right to tell me. I'll see that something's done about it. Meantime, you're not to worry. I can lend you the money quite easily till Mr Merridew pays. I'll go and see him about it.' The Vicar did not add that it would be a pleasure.

'You're too good, sir,' said Mrs Thwaites, 'but I really can't take the money from you, sir. It's Mr Merridew who owes it.'

'That's all right, Mrs Thwaites. It'll just be a loan until he pays. Then you can give it me back.'

'And suppose he doesn't pay, sir?'

'Oh – I'm sure he will. I'll see him myself. If that's no good, there are ways and means of making a man pay – but I'm sure we shan't have to use the law. Now wait a moment while I get my cheque-book.'

Shortly afterwards, Mrs Thwaites left the Vicarage in a

much happier frame of mind, while the Vicar put on his hat in an unusually determined manner and went straight to see Basil. He was in and opened the door. He looked blankly at the Vicar.

'Subscription or something?' he said. 'If so, the answer's no.'

'May I come in for a moment?' asked the Vicar. He was still on the doorstep.

'I suppose so,' said Basil; 'but I'm reading a very interesting book.'

He led the way into the sitting-room, adding as he did so: 'There are no parsons in it.'

The Vicar ignored this remark and said: 'I expect you're surprised to see me.'

'Surprised, yes. Pleased, no.'

'I am no more pleased at having to call on you, but I feel it my duty.'

'Which are you today – a light to guide or a rod to check the erring?'

'Mr Merridew, I repeat that it is no pleasure to me to come to this house now that your nephew has left it.'

'Well – what comes in can go out. You know the way.'

'I shall say what I must and then I shall go.'

'I hope that it will be shorter than your normal sermon – but I don't imagine lack of an audience will deter you.'

'I shall keep my temper, sir,' said the Vicar, rising from his chair, 'because I think you must suffer from some disease of the mind which makes you intolerable to other human beings. You should really be an object of pity.'

'I hope you're not going to cry.'

'Your insults are of the schoolboy variety and I propose to ignore them.'

'If there is a point in your visit – which I'm beginning to doubt – I'm getting a feeling that you just can't wait till

Sunday to preach at someone. Well, I've had quite enough of it, thank you. Go and preach to some of the cattle. They can't answer back.'

'I've come to see you about Mrs Thwaites's bill.'

'Indeed? And what, pray, have you to do with Mrs Thwaites's bill? Have you gone into partnership with her or something? Or perhaps she's going to take up residence at the Vicarage. Really, Vicar, you're a sly devil. No one would have guessed it.'

'Mrs Thwaites is a woman of small means,' began the Vicar.

'But you have enough for two – or more if necessary – though I hardly think that is a likely event –'

'And,' went on the Vicar more loudly, 'she cannot afford to be without her money. You owe her over £30. When are you going to pay her? It's outrageous keeping the poor woman out of it. She's at her wits' end.'

'Since when, Vicar, have you converted yourself into a debt-collecting agency? And what, may I ask, is your commission? The usual ten per cent or a little more, having regard to the quality of the service? With apologies for using the word "service",' he added.

'Very well, sir,' said the Vicar. 'I had hoped that it would not be necessary to say this, but unless this money is paid within three days, solicitors will be instructed to County Court you.'

'Demanding money with menaces, eh? D'you think the Bishop would approve? I had an idea that you could go to prison for quite a long time for that. How awkward it would be for you having to stand to attention for the prison chaplain – a good deal your junior, I expect. Let me see – how does it go? – oh, yes:

'I'd lay down my head
On a hard wooden bed,

And undignified work I'd endure it,
I'd put up with the meals,
But rectorial heels
Will never go click for a curate.'

'This is monstrous. Good day to you, sir,' said the Vicar, and walked out of the room and the house. Never had the Vicar felt as he felt that day. But he was a man of action, and within a very short time of the interview he had repeated the whole story to the General, the doctor, the Gaspards, Colonel Murphy, who was the Chief Constable of Poppleton, and several others. They all agreed that a solicitor should at once be instructed on behalf of Mrs Thwaites to sue Basil in the Poppleton County Court. The General undertook to call on Mr Buckram, the best-known of the Poppleton solicitors.

'Oh, but I must write and demand the money by letter first,' said Mr Buckram, after he had been talking to the General for some minutes.

'Dammit, sir, why?' asked the General. 'You don't write letters to the enemy before firing at him.'

'Ah, but you sometimes ask him to surrender, don't you? It's quite possible that a letter from me will do the trick. That'll save time and money. Besides, my firm has its reputation to think of. There is, of course, nothing illegal in issuing a summons without first demanding the money by letter, but it's unusual and I don't like it. Now, you leave it to me, Sir Bragge, and I think you'll find we soon have Mrs Thwaites's money – unless, of course, he's insolvent. But I expect he's just one of these slow payers. A letter from me will shake his ideas up a bit, as our sergeant-major used to say.'

A few days later Basil received a letter from Mr Buckram demanding the sum of £35 9s. 6d. It should have been £34 18s. 9d., but a slight mistake had been made somewhere, as occasionally happens in the offices of even the most careful solicitor. By return Basil replied:

*I do not owe your client £35 9s. 6d., and what I do owe her will be paid
in my own time. If your client or her reverend and military and medicinal
and other friends want to spend money on litigation, by all means sue.*

Yours faithfully,

Basil Merridew

'What a very unpleasant person,' commented Mr Buckram, after he had read the letter a second time, and he instructed his clerk to issue a default summons for £35 7s. 3d.
for goods sold and delivered, 'particulars of which,' stated
the summons, 'have already been delivered.' They had not
been so delivered and the correct sum of £34 18s. 9d. was not
simply for goods sold and delivered, but included money
paid out on Basil's behalf by Mrs Thwaites for car hire, and
also some charges for laundry work. The amount for goods
sold and delivered should have been £20 3s. 4d. However,
Mr Buckram, like some other solicitors, assumed that it was
all for goods sold and delivered. That's what most of his
clients sued for, and so Mrs Thwaites had to do the same.

The case came on some months later, and it was surprising
how many of the residents round Tapworth Magna managed
to find time to be present. Mr Buckram represented Mrs
Thwaites and Basil appeared for himself. The Judge was
Judge Strachan.

'Thwaites *v.* Merridew,' eventually called the Clerk, and
Mr Buckram rose.

'May it please your Honour,' he began, but the Judge
interrupted.

'Just one moment, please, Mr Buckram,' he said. 'The
Defendant's name seems familiar to me. I think I know him.'

By this time Basil was standing in the witness box. The
Judge looked at him. 'Yes, I do,' he said. 'Have either of you
any objection to my trying this case?'

'None at all, your Honour,' beamed Mr Buckram.

'And you?' queried the Judge to Basil.

'Is there any reason why I should have any objection?' asked Basil innocently.

'That is for you to say,' said the Judge rather tartly.

'I should be delighted for your Honour to try what there is of the case,' replied Basil.

'Very well, then,' said the Judge. 'No, wait a moment,' he added, as he saw Mr Buckram about to begin, and he wrote down in his notebook: 'I state that I know the Deft. No objection by either side.'

'Yes, Mr Buckram,' he said when he had finished.

'May it please your Honour, this is a claim for £35 1s. 8d. for – '

'My copy says £35 7s. 3d.,' interrupted the Judge.

'Oh – I beg your Honour's pardon,' said Mr Buckram. 'Will your Honour forgive me for a moment?' and Mr Buckram started to talk to his clerk about the figures, while the Judge waited patiently. After a minute or two, Mr Buckram returned, not perhaps to the attack, but to a tentative reconnaissance.

'I'm afraid, your Honour, there is a slight confusion with the figures. I don't know whether the Defendant is prepared to admit – ' And he waited hopefully.

'Mr Buckram,' said the Judge a little sternly, 'the Defendant is appearing in person. I don't think he ought to be called upon to make any admissions at this stage.'

'Oh – of course not, your Honour. I shouldn't have suggested such a thing. I was just wondering whether – ' And he paused again, not quite so hopefully. There was silence for a moment or two in Court. As nothing was said, Basil put in:

'Mr Buckram was wondering – or was it wandering, your Honour?'

'Be quiet, sir,' said the Judge, in angry tones. 'Behave yourself, and take your hands out of your pockets.'

'They aren't in my pockets, your Honour. They are

actually hanging down by the sides of my trousers. If your Honour will tell me where you would prefer me to put them, I will willingly carry out your Honour's order – if I can reach.'

'Mr Merridew, you are fined £10 for contempt of Court. If you make one further insolent remark, I shall send you to prison.'

'Your Honour,' said Basil, getting out his pocket-book and starting to count out ten £1 notes.

'Not now,' intervened the Judge. 'Afterwards.'

'I'm sorry, your Honour,' said Basil. 'I assure your Honour that I do not intend any disrespect to the Court and I certainly do not want to be sent to prison, but your Honour mistakenly thought my hands were in my pockets and, to avoid offending your Honour again, I do most respectfully seek direction from your Honour as to where to put my hands.'

'Stand up and behave yourself,' said the Judge, 'and let's have no more nonsense. Yes, Mr Buckram?'

'May it please your Honour, I think I will wait until the witness is in the box before I state the exact amount of this claim. I may have to ask your Honour for an amendment of the Particulars of Claim. I find that apparently, owing to an oversight – '

'One moment, Mr Buckram. Let me see the defence. "I do not owe the Plaintiff £35 7s. 3d." Humph, not very informative, Mr Merridew. How much do you owe?'

'£34 18s. 9d., your Honour.'

'Is that good enough for you, Mr Buckram?'

Greatly relieved, Mr Buckram said: 'Oh yes – certainly, your Honour.'

'How can you pay?'

'In one month.'

'What do you say, Mr Buckram?'

Mr Buckram was so pleased at not having to go into the

figures again that he at once said: 'Oh, yes, your Honour; that is quite satisfactory.'

'Very well, then. Judgement for the Plaintiff for £34 18s. 9d. With costs, I suppose?'

'If your Honour pleases,' said Mr Buckram.

'Who gets the costs?' asked Basil.

'The Plaintiff,' said the Judge.

'Well, if your Honour so directs, of course I shall have to pay, but it does seem to me that I've proved Mr Buckram's case for him. Your Honour will remember we left him wondering.'

'Judgement for the Plaintiff for £34 18s. 9d. with costs payable in one month. Call the next case,' said the Judge.

'Can I give you the £10 now?' asked Basil.

'You will pay that in the office.'

'Very good, your Honour.' Basil left the Court, ignoring the eyes that followed him as he went.

The next day the case was reported in the local newspaper, with the result that several tradesmen in Poppleton, to whom Basil also owed money, rushed round to Mr Buckram and instructed him to issue summonses. In view of the reply to his letter on behalf of Mrs Thwaites, Mr Buckram was prepared to issue the summonses without sending a preliminary demand. In consequence, within ten days of the trial Basil received a number of summonses for amounts which totalled altogether some £80 to £90. The news soon spread round the neighbourhood that Basil was up to his eyes in debt and nearly everyone was delighted. Even the Vicar, who realized that Mrs Thwaites might never obtain her money and might therefore be unable to repay his loan, was in no way disquieted. After his interview with Basil, he contemplated his bankruptcy with some satisfaction. Mrs Stroud alone was on Basil's side. She went over to see him one day. 'People don't like you,' she said, 'and so I expect what I've heard is gross exaggeration, but, if I can be of any help, do please let me. I know it's impertinent of me to suggest it, but I could easily lend you some money if you'd like. I do hope you don't mind my mentioning it.'

'How very sweet of you,' he said. 'But I shouldn't dream of borrowing anything from you or anyone else. I shall stand on my own feet. Don't you worry. But it is kind of you.'

'Well, if you ever change your mind, the offer will still be open.'

'I'm very touched,' said Basil, 'and I won't forget, but it won't be necessary.'

About a month later, Basil again appeared in Court before Judge Strachan. He had paid nothing to Mrs Thwaites and he applied for a further month in which to pay her.

'Your Honour,' he said, 'when I said I could pay in a month I had not had all these summonses. Altogether I've got to find about £150, including the costs. In addition, I've just had to pay some insurance premiums. May I have one more month to pay? I really will square everything up by then.'

'What do you say, Mr Buckram?' asked the Judge.

Mr Buckram was now representing all the creditors, but only Mrs Thwaites so far had obtained a judgement. Acting for her only, he would have refused to consent, but it was to his other clients' interest that he should consent.

'Will your Honour forgive me a moment?' he said, and turned to consult Colonel Murphy, who was the only representative of Mrs Thwaites's supporters present.

'Would you mind if I agreed? It's only one month.'

Colonel Murphy consented and Basil obtained a further month's respite.

'I shall not grant any further time, Mr Merridew,' warned the Judge.

'It will not be necessary, your Honour,' said Basil.

However, the month went on and nothing was paid. The other summonses were due to be heard at the next Court, which was to be held on the last day given to him for payment of Mrs Thwaites's claim. The day in question arrived. Basil had still paid nothing. Colonel Murphy stepped across from the Police Station to see what happened in the other cases. Each one was duly called, but there was no answer to Basil's name.

'Your Honour,' said Mr Buckram, 'I am not altogether surprised at the Defendant's absence. He has not even paid the sum for which your Honour gave judgement two months ago in favour of a client of mine.'

'I remember the case,' said the Judge. 'If my recollection is right, he promised faithfully to pay by today and said that no further time would be necessary.'

'That is so, your Honour.'

'Humph,' said the Judge. 'Well, he still has until half past three.'

'I am not very hopeful, your Honour.'

'Nor am I, Mr Buckram, but stranger things have happened. You'd better prove each of your cases.'

Mr Buckram managed to do so, and the Judge ordered the amounts to be paid forthwith. This meant that theoretically execution could be levied on Basil's goods immediately by the bailiff of the Court. In practice it may take anything up to a week before the bailiff is able to attend to any particular case. Half past three arrived, the Court office closed, and there was still no payment by Basil.

'I wonder if he's run away,' said Colonel Murphy to the General as he reported the news on the telephone.

'I doubt if he could have moved all his things without our hearing of it. Anyway, we shall soon see. The bailiff will be there next week.'

But Basil did not run away, and about six o'clock on the day when all the judgements were given against him he telephoned Mrs Stroud.

'I wonder if I could come and see you at once,' he said.

'Of course.' Mrs Stroud was in fact going to a cocktail party at the Gaspards. Everyone would be there, but she was quite prepared to be late, or even not to go at all, to see Basil.

'I've something rather particular to ask you,' he went on.

'Come right away. I'm glad you haven't forgotten.' Mrs Stroud had heard the news and assumed that he was about to ask for a loan.

'Oh, I'm not coming to borrow anything,' he said.

'Whatever it is, come along at once,' she said, and her heart leaped. Now it is quite true that Basil was very unpopular in the neighbourhood and his behaviour there generally was not that of a man whom many women would even consider as a husband. On the other hand, he was always nice to Mrs Stroud, and little did he know what she had in store for him if and when he had taken her for better and worse. She had been trying to find a new husband for years, ever since the death of her first husband, who had left her some years before he died. She had nearly succeeded several times, but the engagement had been just too long and the suitor had seen a glimpse of what his fate was likely to be. It was a perfectly simple fate – to do, and always to do, what he was told – any revolt being crushed at its inception by Mrs Stroud's own particular methods. Why did she want a husband? She felt incomplete without one and she badly needed a man about the place. When Basil told her that he wanted to speak to her about something particular and that it wasn't a loan, her hopes rose high. She at once sent for the sherry and salted almonds and got out some pistachio nuts – a favourite with Basil. She was already dressed and made-up for the party, but she had another go at her face. She rearranged the cushions on the sofa and then paced up and down the drawing-room, rather like a lioness waiting to be fed.

At last he came. 'I hope it isn't inconvenient,' he began.

'It's never inconvenient,' she said in her softest tones and with her sweetest smile. 'Where will you sit?'

He chose the sofa and she sat next to him.

'It's rather difficult to say,' he said.

This really is it, she said to herself, and conjured up visions of the future.

'I've been wanting to say it for some little time, but I haven't been able to,' he went on.

'I shall love to hear it, whatever it is,' she said, and squeezed his hand.

'Well – it's this – ' He paused for a moment. A delicious moment – there are not so many in one's life. She was glad he paused so that she could enjoy it to the full.

'It's just this,' he repeated. 'I wish you wouldn't always follow me about.'

Mrs Stroud said nothing at first. She thought she must have misheard. Eventually she said: 'What did you say?'

'I'd rather you didn't follow me about.'

Mrs Stroud got up. 'What on earth are you talking about?' she said, her face reddening.

'You must know, my dear,' Basil said quietly, 'you've been following me about ever since I came here. Look at these pistachio nuts. You know how I love them,' and he helped himself to a handful.

'D'you know what you are saying?' she asked. She was not giving up without being absolutely certain.

'Yes, of course, my dear,' he answered. 'I say, these are jolly good.'

'Get right out of my house.'

'I've got to go, as a matter of fact. I must go to the police. But can't I have a glass of sherry first?'

Mention of the police prevented her from simply repeating her order.

'Police? Why?'

'Oh – I've just had a very nasty burglary. I'm on my way to report it.'

'Burglary? Oh – I see – how very convenient, Mr Merridew.'

'Convenient? Damned inconvenient.'

'For the insurance company, perhaps.'

'I say, what an offensive remark. That's really too bad. I certainly shall go. I never expected you to speak like that.'

Basil got up and walked out of the room. As he left, she said: 'And don't ever come back.'

As soon as he had left, her anger, which was still rising, had to find some outlet. 'That bloody man,' she said. 'That bloody, bloody, bloody man.' She repeated the refrain for several seconds. Then she remembered about the burglary. For the moment her mind had been on the phrase, 'I wish you wouldn't follow me about.' The burglary was a tonic. She went to the glass, powdered her face, which badly needed it, and rushed out to get the car. Then she drove it at the most furious speed to the Gaspards. She almost ran into the room where the party was taking place.

'What's the matter, my dear?' inquired Mrs Gaspard.

'That bloody, bloody man,' was all she could say. 'That bloody, bloody man.'

'What man, and what's happened?'

'A drink, please, first. Something strong.' Henry Gaspard came to her aid and she swallowed the first.

'Again, please, Henry. That bloody, bloody man.'

By this time everyone in the room was aware that something had happened and Mrs Stroud became the centre of a most interested circle. It did not take them long to guess that Basil was behind it. After her third drink, she calmed down a bit. Then she prepared them for the news.

'D'you know the latest?'

'No – are the bailiffs in?'

'I don't know – but someone else has been in – or I should say is said to have been in – he's had a burglary.'

'What!'

'He's gone off to report it to the police. What d'you think I said to him? How unfortunate for the insurance company, how convenient for you.'

'How did he like that?'

'He didn't. He went off in a huff.'

'So that's what the trouble's about.'

'Not exactly.' Mention of the cause of the trouble revived memories of 'I wish you wouldn't follow me about'.

'That bloody, bloody man.'

'Tell us some more. What did the burglars take?'

'He didn't say.'

'I bet they've taken his stamp collection,' put in Nicholas. 'He's always boasted how much it's worth, but between you and me it's a lot of rubbish.'

'He'll never get away with it,' put in the doctor. 'It's just too good to be true. When the insurance company gets to know what the position is, they won't stand for it. Just about to have the bailiffs in – and the kindly burglar arrives. How very thoughtful. As you said, Isabel, how very convenient.'

'We must see that he doesn't get away with it,' said the General.

'I think you're right, General,' said the Vicar. He had memories which still rankled. 'How many years can you get for fraud?'

Everyone turned to the Judge.

'I don't think I ought to join this discussion, you know. He may come up before me again.'

So the talk went on, everyone, except the Judge, putting in his or her contribution. Eventually it was just dying down when Colonel Murphy arrived. 'I've got some news,' he almost shouted.

Everyone crowded round while Colonel Murphy told them that Basil had just reported to the police that his house had been broken into and that valuables to the extent of about £3,000 had been stolen.

'Including a stamp collection?' asked Nicholas.

'Including a stamp collection,' said the Colonel, 'value £1,000.'

Talk on the one subject flared up again and the Judge decided he must go.

'Don't be so prim and proper, George,' said the General. 'You're not on the Bench now. How much can you get for fraud?'

'It depends on the kind of fraud. No, I won't be drawn into it. I must leave you to gloat among yourselves, I'm afraid. Anyway,' he could not resist adding, in the tones of Robin Oakapple, 'if a man can't steal his own goods, whose goods can he steal?'

'But a man can't steal his own goods,' came in Dr Sainsbury in the voice of Sir Roderick Murgatroyd.

'A man might try,' said the Judge in the manner of Pooh Bah, and, with that parting shot, he left.

After the Judge had gone, the party grew more hilarious and the fate of Basil was seldom absent from the conversation in at least one part of the room. Meanwhile, Nicholas was drinking rather more than was apparently good for him. Eventually people started to go. Nicholas was one of the last, and he left with Dr Sainsbury, who was also a little the worse for wear.

'I say, Doctor,' he said a little uncertainly, 'don't you think it would be fun to go and commiserate with that jolly old uncle of mine?'

The idea appealed to the doctor, and the two of them went off to find him. The door was open when they arrived, so they walked straight in and found Basil in the sitting-room.

'My poor, poor Uncle,' began Nicholas, 'we have come to weep with you.'

'Nicholas, you're drunk. Get out. Doctor, take him away.'

'My poor Uncle. What does it feel like to be burgled inside out?'

'Are you going, or shall I ring for the police?'

'Police, dear old Uncle? Police? I shouldn't send for them. They might take you away with them. How much did the Judge say he could get?'

'He didn't.'

'Oh – no, I remember – he just said – most reasonably – what was it? – oh, yes, I remember – Gilbert and Sullivan,' and he repeated the dialogue between the Judge and Doctor.

'What else has anybody been saying?'

'Oh, terrible things, my poor, burgled, and over-insured Uncle. The General said – ' and he repeated some of the General's choicer remarks.

'I'm afraid I wasn't too kind myself, dear old Uncle. I spoke about your stamp collection. That was naughty of me, and the old doctor here – well, he did say in the end that you couldn't steal your own goods – which was rather decent of him. Good for you, Doctor.'

For about a quarter of an hour Basil encouraged Nicholas and the doctor to describe in detail the delights of the cock-tail party. When he had heard all he wanted, he said: 'Now, my two young friends, get out and stay out. But you'll hear more of this. There's such a thing as the law of slander in this country.'

T – B

'But not if it's true, venerable Uncle, though now I come to think of it there is something about the greater the truth the greater the libel.'

'Must I throw you out?' asked Basil.

'Come along, Doctor. We're not wanted. *We're* not burglars.'

So the doctor and Nicholas left in not much better condition than when they arrived. Eventually they parted company and Nicholas went to the Vicarage. The Vicar was in the hall. He looked at Nicholas as he stood there swaying, and said: 'I think I should go to bed if I were you.'

Nicholas turned to the Vicar.

'Vicar,' he said, 'dear Vicar. I am very much ashamed – of my uncle,' and collapsed on the floor. The Vicar turned away in disgust, but, finding him still there half an hour later, felt he had no alternative but to put him to bed.

Next morning the atmosphere in the Vicarage was distinctly chilly. Nicholas apologized profusely.

'I'm extremely sorry about last night. It was disgraceful. I'll leave at once and go and stay at the Bear until I can make other plans.'

'I can't pretend I'm pleased,' said the Vicar. 'Your uncle will go to prison and you come home dead drunk. We aren't used to that sort of thing here. But by all means stay a little longer if it will help. I don't want to make too heavy weather of your performance.'

'You have been much too good to me, anyway,' said Nicholas, 'and I can't tell you how sorry I am.'

He left the next day and took a room at the Bear. A few days afterwards a bailiff arrived at Basil's house.

'I'm an officer from the Poppleton County Court,' he said.

'Come in,' said Basil. 'I've been expecting you.'

'I have seven warrants of execution for a total sum of £152 6s. 7d. Can you pay it?'

'I cannot,' said Basil, 'at the moment, but my affairs will all straighten themselves out shortly.'

'I can give you seven days if you'll sign this paper.'

'I'm not sure that seven days will be enough, but let me see the paper.'

He looked at it for a short time and said: 'If I sign this, will you go away?'

'Yes.'

'What will you do if I don't sign it?'

The bailiff hesitated.

'Well?' said Basil. 'If I don't sign it?'

It was an awkward question. In these days County Courts seldom have men to leave in possession of the premises. Legally, the bailiff could have removed the furniture in half an hour, but physically, of course, he could not. If Basil did not sign the paper, he still would have to go away and make arrangements for a van to carry out the removal later.

'Well?' said Basil again. 'You're not very informative.'

'If you don't sign it,' said the bailiff, 'I'm entitled to remove all your goods with certain small exceptions.'

'I see you have an Austin 7 outside. A bit small for the job, isn't it?'

Now, bailiffs are normally resourceful men. They have to be, as they come into contact with a varied assortment of characters. This bailiff was no exception.

'To be quite frank with you, sir,' he said, 'whether you sign the form or not won't make the slightest difference for the moment. I shall have to go away in any event.'

'I see,' said Basil. 'That isn't a great inducement to sign a document by which I see I have to make all sorts of promises.'

'You're perfectly right, sir, and between you and me, if you can find the money within two or three days, you might just as well not sign it. On the other hand, if you can't find the money as quickly, you may find it better to keep me in a good temper. Now, I'm a very normal man and if people make things easy for me, I do what I can for them. Suppose you can't find the money in seven days, then, if you don't sign this form, I shall definitely come along with a van and take your things away to be sold by auction. I shall have to take the risk that you've removed them first. On the other hand, if you sign this form, it's possible – mind you, I'm making no promises – it's possible that I might get you a little longer. Of course, I should have to ask the Plaintiffs' consent to that, but they usually do what I advise. Now, what would you like me to advise them, sir? That you're a reasonable man who, given a little more time, is likely to pay or that you shouldn't be given a minute more than the law allows?'

'Bailiff,' said Basil, 'you ought to have been a barrister. Where do I sign? Oh – I see,' and a moment later he handed the form, duly signed, to the bailiff.

'Thank you very much, sir,' said the bailiff. 'It's an unpleasant job we have to do and it makes it much easier if people see our point of view and are reasonable like you. The law's the law and we have to carry it out – but it's flexible in places.'

'Is it flexible enough,' said Basil, 'to let you join me in a drink?'

Now, whether its flexibility permits such intimacy between bailiff and judgement debtor is uncertain and, therefore, it must remain equally uncertain whether Basil's invitation was accepted. It would be a pity to cast the slightest reflection on an admirable body of men who do their difficult work with great tact, kindness, and good humour.

Shortly afterwards the bailiff left and next day Basil went to London.

Three days later nearly everybody who had attended the cocktail party received a letter from a firm of London solicitors instructed by Basil. The letters varied in their terms, but their effect was that Basil was going to issue a writ for slander against each of the men and women who had suggested that he had been guilty of fraud. Here is the letter which was written to the judge:

His Honour Judge Strachan,
Red Lodge,
Tapworth Magna,
Nr Poppleton, Herts.

Dear Sir, We have been consulted by our client, Mr Basil Merridew. Our client claims that you and a large number of your friends and acquaintances have grossly slandered him by alleging that he staged a false burglary with the intention of defrauding insurance companies. There is no doubt whatever but that there has been a campaign of vituperation directed against our client, culminating in the grave allegations which were made at a party given by Mr and Mrs Gaspard at their house near Tapworth Magna last Thursday. The nature of the slander is so serious and the influence of the persons uttering them so great that it is necessary for our client to take immediate proceedings to clear his name. We wish, however, to give you an opportunity of unreservedly withdrawing and apologizing for the slanders uttered by you. Our client informs us that you yourself did not at first join in slandering him, but that just before you left you made two jests the only innuendo from which was that our client had been guilty of the conduct referred to. The exact words used by you will appear in the Statement of Claim.

We need only add that it is with great personal reluctance that we have to address a letter of this kind to a member of the judiciary, but we hope you will appreciate that the fact that you are such a member makes the damage to our client all the greater.

Within twenty-four hours of the receipt of the letters, a consultation took place at the General's house. It was decided to call in Mr Buckram and an appointment was made with him for the same day. A deputation of the proposed defendants, led by the General, waited on the solicitor. 'Why on earth should we apologize?' said the General. 'It's obvious he's done it. Coincidences like that just don't happen.'

'Undoubtedly,' said Mr Buckram, 'the insurance company will be very suspicious and it will go into the matter very carefully, but it will all take some time.'

'But if we apologize now, we can't say it's true later on,' put in the doctor.

'There is something in that,' said Mr Buckram, 'but equally if you refuse to apologize now the damages – if you lose – will be much heavier.'

'How can we lose if he goes to prison?'

'Oh – you can't lose then.'

'What does the greater the truth the greater the libel mean, then?' put in the doctor.

'Oh, it doesn't refer to slander or civil libel – only criminal libel – which is quite a different matter. You needn't bother about that at all. It's just a question of whether you'll take the risk.'

'What risk?'

'Of not being able to prove that it is a put-up job.'

'The insurance company will prove that.'

'He is insured, I suppose?'

'That's another thing in our favour. He said in Court that he'd just had to pay the premiums. Another unfortunate coincidence.'

'Yes – that is certainly a point in your favour. On the other hand, he says he's definitely issuing writs.'

'He said he was definitely going to pay Mrs Thwaites. He said it twice. He hasn't paid her yet.'

'If you ask me, it's all bluff.'

'Well – there it is, gentlemen, what do you wish me to do – apologize or not?'

'Never,' said the General. 'Do you agree, Doctor? It was all your fault that we're here, anyway.'

'Yes – it was silly of me, I agree, but he'd have been bound to hear about it somehow. There were so many of us involved.

It'll be all round the county by now. Think of the telephone conversations.'

'I fancy Mr Merridew may say something about that when he asks for damages.'

'I tell you it's simply bluff. The man's a cad and a bounder. Look at the way he stood at the wicket until I went out to him.'

'Very well, then, gentlemen. If you are all agreed, I propose to write the following letter. I'll dictate it in your presence. Then, if you don't like it, you can say so.'

He rang for his secretary.

'Take a draft letter, please. To Messrs Groaner and Groaner, 18 Tetbury Street, Strand, w c.

Dear Sirs, I have been consulted by my client – leave the name blank – in regard to your letter of the 19th instant. My client makes no admission that he used the words complained of or that they meant what you allege and he has no apologies to offer. We will accept service of any proceedings you see fit to institute.

'Wait a moment, please, Miss Taylor. How is that, gentlemen? You see, I can't deny that you said the words, because you tell me you did say them, but I can refuse to admit them.'

'Seems quite satisfactory to me,' said the General. ' "He has no apologies to offer." Just right. Dignified. Short. To the point. I say, yes. Anyone against?'

They all agreed and a few days afterwards Mr Buckram accepted service of twenty-two writs for slander.

Meantime, the police had not been altogether idle and, on the day after the writs were received, Detective-Inspector Larch and Detective-Sergeant Gage, at the request of the Chief Constable, called on Basil. They were in plain clothes. He opened the door himself.

'More bailiffs?' he asked politely. 'Come in and have a drink.'

'I am Detective-Inspector Larch and this is Detective-Sergeant Gage.'

'Oh,' said Basil. 'You want some more particulars of the burglary. Please come in.'

He led them into the sitting-room and invited them to sit down.

'Now what further information can I give you, gentlemen?'

'A good deal, please, sir. At the moment all we know is that about 6.15 p.m. on the 13th of this month you reported to the Poppleton police station that £3,000 worth of valuables, including a stamp collection value £1,000, had been stolen. You stated that you had been away for the night of the 12th and, on returning on the 13th, had found the articles missing. You said that you may have forgotten to lock up the house – a very foolish thing to do, if I may say so, sir.'

'You may not say so, Inspector,' said Basil. 'When I require instruction or correction I shall ask for it, and it will not be from you. Kindly reserve your criticisms for those under your immediate command. I am not one of them.'

The inspector flushed. One of these days, he said to himself, when we've got enough evidence to arrest you, I'll make you sorry for that. To Basil he answered: 'We have our duty to do, sir.'

'I don't doubt that,' said Basil. 'I wish you would do it.'

'One of our duties is to advise householders how to behave.'

'That may or may not be the case, but it is my pleasure (I don't consider whether it is my duty) to advise *you* how to behave, and my advice to you, Inspector, is not to begin by making rude remarks to one of your employers.'

Now, if the object of the inspector's visit had simply been for Basil's benefit, to help him recover the property said to have been stolen, he would have left almost at once. But his object was a very different one. So he remained and controlled himself with some difficulty. There was silence for a moment or two. 'You were in the middle of telling me what you knew already, Inspector,' said Basil. 'If you think there is any object to be gained by continuing to tell me what you know and I know and we each know that the other knows, pray continue.'

'You informed us that there were no marks on doors or windows or on the latch that you could see – that was why you thought you must have forgotten to lock up the house. You had left your stamp album lying about the house – ' He paused. He was about to say how foolish that was.

'Yes. Leave out the comment, Inspector, please,' said Basil. 'I will listen to the narrative for what it is worth.' The inspector did not grin, but he bore it. He had his orders.

'You simply found your stamp album, silver, and other articles missing on your return. Detective-Constable Brown came out to your house the same day. He also could find no marks. He saw a number of fingerprints about the house, but they all appear to be your own.'

'Now we are where we started,' said Basil. 'Where do we go from here?'

'I shall be obliged if you will give me much more detail of the articles missing, what they were, where you got them, how much each is worth, how much they're insured for, and so on.' The sergeant got out his notebook.

'Which information would you like first?' said Basil.

'As you please, sir.'

'Very well, then, I'll give you a list of the more valuable stamps. I shall have to lump the others together. It would take too long. Are you ready?'

'Yes.'

'Very well, the most valuable stamp of all is a 5-cent black and white Baltimore 1846 issue which I bought before the war from a small dealer in the South of London who can't have known much about his job. It is catalogued at £250 and worth to me, I suppose, about half as much.'

He then went on to give in detail the descriptions of twenty to thirty stamps of value. By this time the sergeant was getting a little tired of writing and the inspector of listening.

'Are there many more?' he asked.

'Oh, yes,' said Basil. 'I've a very good memory for them, you know. Most collectors have.'

We shall be here all day at this rate, thought the inspector.

'Haven't you a duplicate of the claim you've submitted to the insurance company? That would save a lot of time.'

'I dare say it would,' said Basil, 'but they're not insured.'

'Not insured?' said the inspector incredulously.

'No.'

'I suppose the policy excluded stamps, then?'

'I haven't a policy. None of my things are insured. That's why I'm so worried about the loss.'

The inspector and the sergeant looked at each other. If that was true, their errand was hopeless. 'But I was told,' said the inspector, 'that you had recently mentioned the payment of insurance premiums. Perhaps you weren't able to pay them and the policies lapsed?'

'I don't know who told you that or what business it is of yours or anyone else's to pry into my affairs, but the only policies I have are life policies. It is quite true that I did refer at the County Court to the payment of premiums on these policies. I suppose the Chief Constable told you. I saw him sitting there lapping it all up. I hope he'll be as pleased when he's sitting in the High Court as a defendant himself. Now, what more can I do for you, gentlemen?'

It was quite plain to the inspector that there was nothing more to be done. It could be ascertained whether Basil was telling the truth and, if he was not in fact insured, any suggestion of a bogus burglary was ludicrous. As far as tracing the thief or thieves was concerned, he had all the information he needed. He had come for evidence to put Basil in the dock. He had only succeeded in obtaining evidence which, if true, would most certainly keep him out of it. Accordingly, he made a few more perfunctory inquiries and ended by asking if a list of the missing articles could be forwarded at Basil's convenience.

'It's funny how you seem to have lost interest in the case since I told you I was uninsured,' said Basil. 'A more suspicious person than I might have thought that the object of your visit was not to help me get back my property, but to prove I hadn't lost any. No doubt the Chief Constable would have preferred it that way, considering what he's said about me. However, that's not your concern, Inspector, is it? As far as I know, you haven't said anything about me yourself yet, and, if I were you, I shouldn't. It's going to prove very expensive for those who have.'

'It's not part of my duty to listen to your offensive observations about my superiors,' said the inspector, getting up to go.

'No,' said Basil; 'though it apparently is your duty to try to obtain evidence for the benefit of your superiors' private litigation. At any rate, you have spent part of this afternoon in doing so. Or should I say wasted?'

'Good afternoon, sir,' said the inspector.

'You can find your way out, Inspector. Don't leave any fingerprints on the door, please. It might be so confusing for the next police officer who arrives.'

It was not long before the dreadful news that Basil was not insured went all round Tapworth Magna. Mr Buckram, however, when consulted, said it would be best to make inquiries before taking any decisive step in the matter. Two or three weeks later at another meeting at his office he announced the doleful news to a deputation from the defendants that Basil had no policy on any of his belongings.

'Well,' said the General, 'it's no good sitting down and crying. What do we do now? We must make a plan.'

'It is clearly a case where we must take counsel's opinion,' said Mr Buckram. 'I will instruct my London agents to arrange a consultation with the two best-known authorities on libel and slander in the Temple.'

A week later Mr Buckram, the General, the doctor, Nicholas, and a representative of Mr Buckram's London agents, Mr Pound, attended a consultation with Mr Adam Twigg, Q.C., and Mr Rowland Stewart.

Mr Twigg was a man of few words – unlike some of his learned colleagues – and his opinions were, whenever possible, quite definite. He had the courage of his convictions. He never wrote, for instance: 'While, of course, it is possible that the Court might take a different view and while much depends on the evidence of Mr Crookshank, I think on the whole that, etc., etc. I must, however, make one or two reservations, first, etc., etc.' He informed his client what the law was, occasionally adding that there was a decision to the contrary, but that it was wrong. He had to be rather more guarded on questions of fact, but even there he had almost a woman's intuition not necessarily for the truth, but for the probable result.

'Well,' he said, 'this is a nice kettle of fish. There's no defence to the actions. It's only a question of damages. They'll be heavy. A doctor, the local Vicar, the Chief Constable, a County Court Judge, a former High Sheriff of the county, the man's own nephew – dear, dear, dear. You must apologize at the earliest possible moment and see how much he'll take. If you can't settle, we must make a payment into Court. We must get the actions consolidated if possible and

then pay in an amount which will make him think before he
refuses it.'

'What sort of amount have you in mind?' asked Mr
Buckram.

'Humph,' said Mr Twigg. 'It's a very serious slander. The
plaintiff may have to give up his house and leave the neighbourhood. It's not like a few words of abuse from a fishwife,
though, if I may say so, as little care seems to have been taken
before the words were used. Let me see. Twenty-two defendants. A refusal to apologize in the first instance. The most
he's likely to get altogether is £20,000, the least £5,000.
Juries vary. I can't be more definite than that. I should pay
in £7,500. A settlement at £10,000 would be reasonable,
but I don't think he'd risk going on with that amount
in Court and the offer of a public apology. D'you agree,
Stewart?'

'Entirely.'

'Anything you'd like to ask?' said Mr Twigg.

'It seems a great deal of money,' said the General, when
he had got his breath back.

'It *is* a great deal of money,' said Mr Twigg, 'and it will be
free of tax. If I may say so, however, you should have thought
of that before you made wholesale allegations against the
man, however much you dislike him. Burglars *may* arrive
when a person is up to his eyes in debt. Coincidences *do*
happen. I once heard a witness say: "May God strike me
dead if I'm telling a lie." The next moment he had collapsed.
Every one was frozen for a few seconds. Then they went to
his assistance. He wasn't dead – just a faint, but he ought to
have been: he'd been lying like a trooper.'

Mr Twigg was talking rather more than usual. This was
because, in spite of his rather brusque manner, he was quite
a kindly man and wanted to give the unfortunate defendants
a little more of his time for their money.

'How do you suggest we approach him?' asked Mr Buckram.

'In the usual way, I suppose. But no. I think you might ask his solicitors if he'd consent to receive a deputation from the defendants without prejudice. Send an open apology first, of course. But you never know with a chap like this. You may find that, if his solicitors will let you approach him personally, he'll respond more readily. You can never tell. He might even take £500. But you must feel your way carefully. Try and get him to mention the sort of figure he has in mind first. If he's thinking of £5,000 and you offer £500, it'll only put his back up. You say he's a difficult chap. He may, of course, refuse to see you. In that case, Mr Buckram or Mr Pound must do his best with the plaintiff's solicitors. I'm sorry to be so pessimistic, gentlemen, but it's better to know it now than when you hear the jury's verdict.'

'Mr Twigg,' said the General, 'I'm sure you'll forgive me, but I'm a plain man and say what I think. Is there any possibility that your judgement is wrong? I have myself made mistakes on the field of battle.'

'So has everyone,' replied Mr Twigg, 'including me, of course. But not in this case. It's too plain. You want to know why? All right. First question: Did you speak the words complained of? Answer: Yes. Second question: Did the words impute a criminal offence to the plaintiff? Answer: Yes. Third question: Were they uttered on what we call a privileged occasion – that is to say, had you any duty or right to talk as you did? Answer: No. Fourth question: Can you prove the words to be true? Answer: No. Only remaining question: What are the damages? Well, there I've had to leave a wide margin, but I cannot see any jury giving less than £5,000 all told. People in your position cannot combine to take away a man's character without paying heavily for it. No: it seems to me a clear case. Of course, if you query the answers to any of the questions I've posed, that would be different. But can you? Could you yourselves answer any of the five questions differently? I may add that I have discussed the matter with my junior, Mr Stewart, who has vast experience in these cases, and he is of exactly the same opinion.'

'Exactly,' said Mr Stewart.

Nicholas had so far said even less than Mr Stewart. 'I think the idea of a deputation to my uncle is excellent,' he put in, 'though I'd better not form part of it myself. I was pretty offensive to him on the last occasion we met, as far as I remember. But he's a man of very queer moods. Mr Twigg is quite right. Approached in the proper way, he might take £500 or even less. He's a very difficult man to handle, but, if you get him in the right temper and make the right approach, you can do quite a lot with him.'

'Well,' said Mr Twigg, 'that seems the best bet. Now, are there any more questions?' There were not, and the unhappy little party returned to Tapworth Magna.

'Chin up,' said the General on the way home when the conversation flagged. 'We must decide who's to be in the deputation.' They were wasting their time, however, in that respect, as Basil's solicitors replied to the apology and the suggestion of a meeting between the parties without prejudice as follows:

We are obliged for your letter of the 1st instant on which we have taken our client's instructions. He notes that your clients now wish to apologize and to see him with a view to compromising the matter. Without at present inquiring into the reasons for your clients' sudden change of front, our client desires us to say that he will be quite prepared to meet a 'without prejudice' deputation of the defendants consisting of the following: General Sir Bragge Purbrick, His Honour Judge Strachan, Dr Sainsbury and the Reverend Maitland Temperley. We should emphasize that he will not be prepared to discuss the matter with anyone except these four gentlemen and, if this is not satisfactory to your clients, the matter must take its normal course.

Basil had foreseen that neither the Vicar nor the Judge would have come willingly.

A meeting was duly arranged and, on the day before, a consultation was held of all twenty-two defendants. The General, as usual, took the chair.

'The object of this meeting,' he said, 'is to see how much each of us can pay. We shall assume the worst and if, as I hope, that does not happen, the amounts will be scaled down accordingly. Any objections to this course?'

There were none.

'Very well, then,' went on the General. 'Let us assume that the damages are £20,000.' A shudder ran through his audience. 'That was the maximum figure mentioned by Mr Twigg – a man, if I may say so, after my own heart. Now, there are twenty-two of us, but our financial position varies and I think that each man should give as he is able. Take the Judge, for instance. Can you manage £500?'

'£500,' cried the Judge. 'A County Court Judge can't spare that out of his salary.'

'A County Court Judge can try,' put in the doctor.

The Judge did not laugh. It was the first time that a quotation from the source in question had fallen flat.

'Well – how much, then?' asked the General.

'I haven't anything to spare at all,' said the Judge. 'I find it difficult to make ends meet as it is. I've a wife, and two children at school. I'm paying £250 a year on my house, £100 insurance premiums – I'm overdrawn at the bank. I really don't know what I can do.'

The Judge began to have even more sympathy than usual for the debtors who appeared before him and said they were unable to pay.

'What about your capital position?'

'My capital position? Look here, I'm not going to be cross-examined as though I were in the witness box asking for time to pay.'

'But my dear George,' said the General, 'there's nothing to be ashamed of. Think of the cases which came before you when we were in Court.'

'I prefer not to,' said the Judge. 'I might manage a couple of hundred pounds, but with great difficulty.'

'Very well, then, that will do for a start,' said the General. 'Judge Strachan, £200. Now, Dr Sainsbury?'

'£500.'

'Good. Nicholas?'

'£250.'

'Right. Henry?'

'£3,000, if necessary.'

So they went on and, in the end, after a few adjustments, they reached the figure of £20,000.

'Excellent,' said the General. 'Now we can go into battle knowing we have the weapons.'

'I'm not at all sure that I'm liable at all,' said the Judge. 'I only quoted a couple of lines of Gilbert. Everyone knows I'm always doing that.'

'Yes, but what lines? Anyway, Mr Twigg had no doubt about it.'

'Did you ask him about my case specifically?'

'No, I can't say we did, but he and Stewart had all the papers and both said there was no defence to any of the actions.'

'Well, I think I shall go up to Town and see an old friend of mine at the Bar. If I'm liable, of course I'll stand in with you and, if absolutely necessary, produce £200. But if I'm not liable I don't see why I should.'

'Fair enough,' said the General. 'When will you let me know the result?'

'I'll go up tomorrow and phone you in the evening.'

The next day Judge Strachan managed to obtain an interview with a well-known junior at the Bar, Humphrey Maynard.

'Hullo, old boy,' said Maynard, 'what brings you to Town? Not enough judgement debtors in the country?'

'I want some advice.'

'Point of law too difficult for you, I suppose, and you've reserved judgement?'

'Nothing of the kind. It's a personal matter.'

'Oh dear. Not driving under the influence, I hope.'

'It isn't funny at all, old man.'

'Oh – I'm sorry. What is it?'

The Judge gave Maynard the details and then asked: 'D'you think I've any defence?'

'Well, I don't do much libel, you know, and if Twigg and Stewart say you haven't, I shouldn't have thought you had.'

'But I was only making a sort of joke. I didn't say a word against him till then.'

'I know, but how were your words understood? That's the test, isn't it? Did they make people think you were falling into line with the others and calling the fellow a crook? Look here, if you like, and don't mind my telling him, I'll ask Clapson to come in. He knows all about these things.'

'Do,' said the Judge. He would have told his trouble to the whole of the Bar if it would have done any good.

'Ask Mr Clapson if he could spare a moment,' said Maynard on the internal telephone to his clerk. 'Thank you.'

A few minutes later Clapson came in. The Judge and he were not personally known to one another, Clapson's practice only having developed after the Judge had gone to the Bench. As soon as they were introduced, however, 'Oh dear,' said Clapson, 'I'm afraid I know what you're here for, Judge. I'll have to go out again. I'm afraid I'm just settling a Statement of Claim against you.'

'Oh, good Lord,' said the Judge.

'Slander action. Twenty-two defendants. That's it, isn't it?'

'Yes, I'm afraid so. I just came in to see what Maynard thought my chances were.'

'Well, Judge, if you really want me to, I don't mind telling you what I think,' said Clapson. 'It won't be giving away any confidences.'

'Well?' said the Judge.

'Nil,' said Clapson. 'It's an open and shut case. Horrible position for you, Judge. I'm so sorry. I hope it's settled – should hate to have to cross-examine you. Most embarrassing.'

'What d'you think the damages will be, then? Or would you rather not say?'

'Well – I oughtn't to mention figures, in case you've a larger one in mind, Judge, but heavy, very heavy.'

'Against me?'

'Against all of you. The plaintiff seems a decent enough chap, bit short of money, of course, but –'

'A decent enough chap, did you say?'

'Yes, he seemed all right to me, Judge; but I gather he's not very popular in the neighbourhood.'

'He's an out-and-out bounder.'

'Clapson thinks all his geese are swans,' put in Maynard. 'That's one of his few failings. So I shouldn't worry about that.'

'But,' he added after Clapson had left them, 'the trouble seems to be that it doesn't much matter what the plaintiff's like. It's damned bad luck, though. I wish I could be of more help.'

The Judge returned disconsolately to Tapworth Magna and telephoned the General.

'I'll pay,' he said resignedly. 'But try and keep it as low as possible.'

'You'll be there yourself,' said the General.

'Oh, of course,' said the Judge.

On the following Wednesday the required deputation met at Basil's house. He greeted them with surprising cordiality. 'Come in, my dear fellows,' he said. 'Nice to see you all. Quite a long time since we met. Oh, this is Mr Mountain of the Poppleton County Court,' and he introduced them all to the bailiff. 'Suppose we have a drink first of all. What for you, General?'

This was a very different atmosphere from what had been expected, but, although they would not in the normal way willingly have drunk with Basil, there was plainly no alternative. Moreover, their hopes began to rise. Nicholas had said Basil was a man of many moods. Perhaps they had arrived at the psychological moment.

'I suppose one of you couldn't lend me £155?' he asked.

'Certainly, my dear fellow,' said the General. 'Delighted. When would you like it?'

'Well, it's Mr Mountain here who wants it, really. Will you take a cheque, Mr Mountain?'

'Well, I can't really sir. But I tell you what I can do for you, if you like. It's a little irregular, but – '

'Within the flexibility of the law,' prompted Basil.

'Exactly, sir. If Sir Bragge is prepared to give me his open cheque on a Poppleton Bank, I will go and cash it myself and pay it into the County Court.'

'That's uncommonly civil of you,' said Basil. 'What do you say, General?'

'Only too pleased. Just wait while I get out my cheque book.'

It was not long before the bailiff was on his way back to Poppleton.

'Perhaps I can repay the loan by bringing it into account in the little matter you've come to discuss?'

'Certainly, my dear fellow.'

'Judge, your glass is empty. There. That's better. And you'll be pleased to see I haven't got my hands in my pockets.'

Judge Strachan grinned feebly.

'And I'm standing up straight too.'

The Judge tried again, but it was not very successful.

'Well, now, what's the news?' said Basil genially to the company in general. 'How's my rascal of a nephew? He was half seas over last time I saw him.' So the conversation went on for about twenty minutes. Then the General fired a sighting shot.

'Now, my boy,' he said, in a jovial tone. 'What about our little dispute? It's good of you to see us.'

'Not at all, my dear General, not at all. Only too pleased. It's such a pity you're not paying just a friendly call. I should have preferred that.'

'Well, it's fairly friendly at the moment,' said the doctor.

'And no reason, I hope, why it shouldn't continue to be so,' said Basil.

By this time hopes had risen considerably higher and looks were exchanged between the members of the deputation which indicated as much.

'Vicar, another glass of sherry? How are the sermons going? Anyone listening yet?'

'As usual, thank you.' There was a limit beyond which the Vicar would refuse to go, but he was prepared to suffer to a certain extent for the general good.

'I say, old man,' said Basil to the Judge, 'I suppose you couldn't lend me £10. That £10 you fined me put me back a bit. I'm not a wealthy chap like you.'

The General glared at the Judge. He was quite plainly giving an order. For once, the law felt it had to obey. With as good a grace as possible, the Judge started to extract ten one-pound notes from his pocket-book.

'No – not now, Judge, please. Afterwards. What does it feel like to be at the receiving end?' he added. If the Judge had not been so extremely anxious to keep the damages down to a minimum he would have walked out of the house, or, at least, tried to make some effective retort. As it was, he could only resort to another attempt at a grin. It made him look as if he were going to be sea-sick – but for his colour, which was red rather than green.

'What fun it must be being a Judge,' said Basil. 'No one can contradict you. Everyone has to do what you tell him. Now, do take this chair, Judge. I particularly want you to sit here.' And the Judge sat.

'Now gentlemen,' said Basil, 'I think it very kind of you to come to see me. It must have cost some of you quite a lot – not in money, I mean – yet.'

The General decided to make a small reconnaissance. 'Now, my dear Merridew, I'm a plain man. We're in the wrong – and we want to say we're sorry, damnably sorry. Forgive me, Vicar.'

'That's very generous of you, General. I wonder if each of the others would mind repeating that. Please don't if you'd rather not. Vicar?'

The Vicar swallowed. 'I offer you my unreserved apologies,' he said.

'Judge?'

'I, too,' said the Judge.

'That's not very liberal,' said Basil. 'Is that all you want to say?'

'I'm extremely sorry,' said the Judge, 'and I withdraw the allegations unreservedly.'

'That's much better,' said Basil. 'I'd like to remember that. Would you mind repeating it?'

The Judge hesitated, but his financial position was undoubtedly very bad and he did as he was asked.

'Just once more to please me,' coaxed Basil.

When the apologies were over, the General tried again.

'We've done you a wrong, Merridew, and we want to put it right. I don't suppose you want money, but, if you do, tell us how much and we'll see if we can agree.'

'You go so fast,' said Basil. 'I'm a lonely man and it's such a change having you here. If we agree at once, I'm sure you'd all go away. Another drink?'

They had to humour him and dropped the subject.

After another quarter of an hour, Basil said: 'It isn't fair to keep you in suspense like this. I'm so sorry. I'm being selfish. And, after all, I know the way these things happen. Walk into any club in London and hear what they're saying. Enough material for fifty slander actions.'

'I'm so glad you see it in that light,' said the doctor.

'How could you tell that I wasn't insured? How could you know that my house really had been burgled? You couldn't. Appearances were all against it.'

'You take a very generous view,' said the General.

'You have a very liberal mind,' added the Vicar.

'I very much appreciate your attitude,' said the Judge, feeling on firmer ground.

'But, of course,' went on Basil, 'the law – ass that it is – says nothing about not knowing, does it, Doctor?'

The doctor made no answer. He realized what was coming.

'Or taking a generous view, General?'

The General was silent.

'Or having a liberal mind, Vicar?' He paused, and then added: 'Or much appreciating an attitude, Judge? Of course, it should do, Judge. But it doesn't, Doctor. But don't worry. I shan't take any notice of anything any of you have said – tonight.'

There was silence for a moment. The Judge and the doctor, with their knowledge of Gilbert and Sullivan, knew that their mission had failed. The General and the Vicar did not recognize the use of *The Mikado*, but they did realize that the battle was lost.

'Now, about your execution,' continued Basil. 'Will £15,000 suit you?' There was no answer. 'Come, gentlemen, don't I hear £15,000?' He turned to the General. 'What about you, sir? It's a good case, no flaws in it, guaranteed impregnable against any attack – what do I hear then? Won't someone start the bidding?' Still no sound.

'I should have mentioned that there's a reserve.'

'How much?' said the General.

'£10,000.'

The General looked at the others. 'We'll pay,' he said.

A week later all twenty-two actions were settled and Basil was paid £10,000, less the £165 he had borrowed at the meeting. He graciously agreed to give credit for that sum. Nicholas insisted on paying to the Vicar the amount of the latter's contribution. 'I feel in a way responsible,' he had said. Everyone thought it was a fine gesture on his part, but this in no way mollified the feelings of his uncle's victims towards Basil, nor did the fact that he agreed to forgo a public apology on the ground that it would only give more publicity to the slanders, nor did the sale of his house and his early departure from the neighbourhood. He had played with the deputation unmercifully, and, as Mr Twigg had agreed, £10,000 is a lot of money.

The anger of the defendants remained intense for some time, but it was nothing to what it would have been if they had happened to look inside the first-class Pullman car of a train leaving London some weeks later. Basil was in it and, if they had followed him on his way there, they would have been puzzled at his behaviour, so different from his manners at Tapworth Magna. He apologized to a man who had carelessly bumped into him, he helped an old lady with her luggage, and he gave five shillings to the porter who carried his. But it was not only Basil they would have seen in the restaurant car. Opposite him was Nicholas.

'We shan't be able to do that again, old boy,' he was saying. 'However far away we went, there might be someone who had a friend at Tapworth or who somehow had heard of us. Much too risky.'

'I quite agree, old man,' said Basil. 'But I've been thinking things over the last two or three days, and what d'you say to this?'

He then started to unfold to Nicholas another plan for making money without giving anything appreciable in return. After he had listened for some time, Nicholas interrupted: 'But we can't do that.'

'Why not, old man?' asked Basil, surprised.

'Illegal, old boy,' said Nicholas.

Chapter 2

OPERATION ENTICEMENT

———

A SURE sign of poverty among the sometimes well-to-do is the half-bottle of gin, and that is all that Basil's wife, Elizabeth, could find in the cupboard. There was not very much in it. Now supposing, she said to herself, I have a small one now – just a very small one – will there be enough when Basil comes home with Nicholas and Petula? Even on the most conservative estimate of their requirements, it was obvious that there would not. 'Requirements', by the way, is the right word. Basil was, of course, entitled to 'require' in his own home while Nicholas and his wife, Petula, who had the flat next door, lived on what was almost a communal basis with Basil and Elizabeth. They shared pretty well everything together, money, food, clothes, ideas, happiness, disappointments, and, at the moment, poverty. Elizabeth sighed and helped herself, and, as a small one would leave too little in any event, she took a large one. They will understand, she said to herself; they will have to. She was a lovely creature and could obtain almost anything from anyone who did not know her well and from some who did. She combined the languorous beauty of a South American film star with an almost perpetually puzzled look. 'It is all so difficult,' she seemed to say. 'Won't you help me?' If any man could resist her face and figure – and, if he was normal, this was not easy – the little frown would usually finish him. Basil and Elizabeth in their poorer times owed quite a number of good dinners from wealthy strangers to this little frown. To do them justice, they did not particularly care for dinners of this kind – or, more accurately, they liked the dinners all right, but preferred their own company. However, one must eat, they consoled themselves. And drink, sighed Elizabeth, as she took another one. The absence of inverted commas from Elizabeth's thoughts is not accidental. She said very little out loud either to herself or other people. It was her expression which answered you, sometimes accompanied by a low, drawling murmur. So very different from Petula, who was pretty, inclined to be pert, and who talked incessantly. Basil and Nicholas rarely listened to her, but she did not mind. She prattled on gaily, very occasionally slowing down the pace as if to say: 'Now, this is important; you must listen to this.' The change in tempo often had the desired effect.

I wonder, thought Elizabeth, if Petula has any left. I'll go and see. She had the key to their flat and went to look. While she was there, Basil came back with Nicholas and Petula. As usual, Petula was talking.

'The first was a fault, at least Nicholas called "Fault". As a matter of fact, I wasn't absolutely certain if it was a fault. You know it's sometimes awfully difficult to see on the Browns' court. Anyway, after Nicholas had called "Fault" – '

'Petula,' said Nicholas, pleasantly, 'could you pipe down for just a moment?'

'Darling,' said Petula, 'I'm so sorry. I won't say another word for five minutes – or do I mean five seconds? It's funny what an awful long time even a second is, while a minute, if you really stop and count it, seems like hours. I remember once . . .'

'Oh, Petula,' said Nicholas.

'How would it be if you bought me one of those things they used to put on a scold's mouth? I remember seeing a picture in a book in that hotel we were staying at – now where was it – wasn't it in the Lake District – ?'

'Don't start talking about hotels,' said Basil. 'I'm beginning to think we shall never see the inside of one again – except the sort which has up in large letters outside "FOR GENTLEMEN ONLY", and spells "accommodation" with one m. Hell, there's hardly any gin left. Elizabeth,' he called. She returned from her fruitless search a few minutes later.

'I'm sorry,' said Nicholas. 'We had the last drop yesterday.'

'Now,' said Basil firmly, 'we've got to do something. I'm tired of this. Not enough to eat, not enough to drink, no theatres, hardly a cinema, no holidays, no riding, no golf. Yes, I know,' he added to Elizabeth, who, without saying a word, indicated that 'you have us.' 'But you can't live on caviare.' Elizabeth gave him a look which, five years before, would have made up for the shortage of gin.

'I quite agree with you, old man,' said Nicholas. 'Things are getting out of hand. We'd better make an appreciation.'

Two years previously Basil and Nicholas, posing as uncle and nephew, had set out together, without their wives, to make their fortunes and, it must be conceded, that they had not done at all badly out of Tapworth Magna. Elizabeth and Petula had been a little against their husbands going away for so long, and Basil himself, who had worked out the idea of 'The Disagreeable Man', had considered the risk of leaving the lovely Elizabeth. Their circumstances were such, however, that they could not afford to be too particular, and the idea seemed such a good one that they had all decided to take a chance on it. Their reunion after the reduction of Tapworth Magna was a very happy one. Basil described Mrs Stroud to Elizabeth in terms which made her very happy. Elizabeth described no one to Basil. Petula and Nicholas discussed their respective tennis parties, and Petula talked so much that Nicholas did not seem to get a chance to mention Barbara Newton – not a reasonable chance, anyway. But the champagne had long been drunk, some of the trinkets, with which Basil and Nicholas loved to adorn their wives after a successful adventure, had already found their way back to the places from which they came or very similar places, and the £10,000, which seemed so large when it arrived from Mr Buckram, had shrunk to an almost unbelievable extent. The danger – which so far they had usually managed to avoid – the danger of having to earn an honest living by hard work started to appear horribly close. The almost empty half bottle of gin was a very real warning.

To do Basil and Nicholas justice, it would not have been particularly easy for them to find an ordinary job. Admittedly, they did not like work, but, apart from purely manual labour, of which they had no experience, there was little employment for which they were suited. They could each have advertised at the end of the 1939–45 War that they were ex-majors with administrative ability and that they sought interesting and remunerative posts. They did not, however, waste their money. They were not prepared to hawk round vacuum-cleaners. During the war Basil had somehow or other collected a D.S.O. and Nicholas an M.C., and this, added to their public school education and the other attributes already mentioned, made them virtually unemployable. Brains they had, as their first exploit since the war showed, but that was very nearly all they had – besides, of course, their wives.

'Well, there's no doubt about our object,' said Basil. 'We can skip that. Considerations. Well, between us, I should say we have about £500 all told – '

'And some pawn-tickets,' put in Nicholas.

'Don't remind me,' said Petula. She had enjoyed her fur coat while it lasted.

'Our rent is paid for the next quarter. We have nothing

more to sell. Now, courses open. We can try to get a job.'

'Hopeless.'

'Right. That's out. We can steal.'

'Too difficult and too dangerous. Too much risk for too little.'

'That's out.'

'We can borrow.'

'Only from each other. So that's out.'

'We can send our wives to work.'

'Really!' said Petula.

What, me? looked Elizabeth.

'What can they do?'

'We ought to be able to make use of them. Elizabeth is beautiful, Petula is pretty, both have legs which in some professions would be worth quite a lot of money.'

'That's coarse,' said Petula. 'Don't.'

Mine *are* rather lovely, looked Elizabeth.

'Humph,' said Basil, 'we *ought* to be able to do something with them. As a matter of fact, I've been toying with an idea for the last day or two. It'll take a bit of time, though. Wait a moment.'

The others watched him. Even Petula was quiet. She was trying to remember how much it would cost to get back the fur coat.

'The Sunday papers,' said Basil after a little. 'Did you see Mrs Blarney's life story the other day? I bet they paid her a bit for that. And she was ugly as sin.'

'I don't follow,' said Nicholas.

'A beautiful woman with a story can sell it.'

'Do you know any stories about me?' said Elizabeth.

'No – but we can make one.'

'How?'

'That's the trouble. It'll take a bit of time.'

'Tell us.'

'Well, you know that divorce cases can't normally be reported.'

Oh, not a divorce, please, looked Elizabeth.

'Of course not, silly. Not even a pretence of one. But other people's domestic affairs still get the best publicity. Look at the space given to a fruity breach of promise action.'

'Well?'

'Well now, although the Press can't report divorce cases, they can report enticement actions, and if one or other or both of you girls were involved in one, they jolly well would.'

'I see light,' said Nicholas. 'Who's to seduce whom?'

'The word is "entice", not "seduce". Now, enticement actions are not looked on with favour by the Courts because in the ordinary husband and wife case the Divorce Court is available, and judges and juries no doubt think that the only reason for bringing an enticement action instead of a divorce case is to get publicity. In other words, legal blackmail. But if someone takes away someone else's wife without seducing her, then there'd be no ground for a divorce case – not for three years, anyway – but there would be ground for an enticement action.'

'So you mean,' said Nicholas, who was never very far behind once the seed was sown – 'that one of us takes away the other's wife, that we have an enticement action, full of fruity incidents and that then our wives sell their life stories to the papers.'

'And we too, I dare say,' said Basil. 'We can't make a fortune, but, if we play our cards well, we should do quite decently out of it. Of course, we'll have to find the legal expenses, which'll be quite a bit, and we'll have to live until the case is over, but I reckon we can just about do that on what we've got. We'll have to go carefully, though. Now, what d'you all say?' They talked it over at length and the more they did so the better it seemed.

'We've got to make it really alive,' said Basil. 'When we give evidence we've got to know our facts, and we'll have to have some genuine independent evidence as well.'

'So we'll have to go through all the motions, you mean,' said Nicholas.

'Exactly. My case will be that you, my oldest friend, have deliberately set out to steal my wife from me, with the result that eventually she leaves me and goes to live with you and Petula. Your case will be that I'm a brute of a husband who's driven my wife away. Petula will stand up for you. We must act all the scenes, even the ones between ourselves.'

'How lucky,' said Nicholas, 'that you're not going to allege misconduct between me and Elizabeth.'

'Yes,' said Basil. 'And don't either of you forget it.'

Elizabeth looked, how could you? And Petula said: 'You can rely on me.'

So they voted for the plan and went into it in great detail. It was like making the scenario for a play. Basil and Nicholas were both quite right in insisting that they should play their parts in full throughout. Giving evidence of things which haven't happened is a very difficult task indeed. If, however, you actually have done the things of which you are speaking, it is comparatively easy, even if, as in the present case, it was all (as between the main actors) only part of a play.

A week later Mr Brian Mallet, a young solicitor who had not long been admitted, received a new client, Mr Basil Merridew. Clients were so scarce for Mr Mallet that he did not even dare to keep Mr Merridew waiting in case he went away. It was not due to any lack of ability that Mr Mallet had few clients, but simply to inexperience and the lack of enough influential friends. He would have been wiser to have taken a position as managing clerk for a year or two, but he was of a very independent mind, he hated receiving orders, and he liked to be on his own. Basil had chosen him out of the *Law List* as one of the most recently admitted solicitors practising by himself.

'Mr Basil Merridew, sir,' announced the shorthand-typist-cashier-managing-clerk-and-office-boy.

'Please come in and sit down, sir,' said Mr Mallet. 'What can I do for you?'

'Thank you. I'm in a bad way. May I smoke, please?'

'Of course. Please have one of mine. What is the trouble?'

'Terrible. I don't find it easy to talk about.'

'I quite understand. Please take your time.'

'Are you a married man, if you'll forgive me asking?' said Basil.

'Not yet.'

'Then you won't be able to understand. I hope you never will.'

Mr Mallet looked sympathetic. 'I'm terribly sorry. Try to tell me about it. Your wife has left you for another man?'

Basil looked surprised. 'That's very quick of you.'

'It's my job. How long has it been going on?'

'I can't say exactly. I wouldn't have believed it possible. It's my oldest friend who's done it, damn him – but I'll get her back yet.'

'Then you've not come for a divorce?'

'Not if I can help it. Anyway, there are no grounds – none that I can prove at the moment.'

'Where is your wife now?'

'She's gone to live in his flat.'

'Grounds enough for divorce, I should say, if you want it.'

'His wife is there too.'

'Oh, I see. That does make a difference. Please tell me all about it from the start.'

T–C

Half an hour later Mr Mallet, in Basil's presence, dictated the following letter to Nicholas:

Dear Sir, I have been consulted by my client Mr Basil Merridew in regard to his domestic affairs. My client informs me that as a direct and intended result of your behaviour his wife has left him and gone to stay with you and your wife. Our client is devoted to his wife and is desperately anxious for her to return. I am, therefore, to request you to ask Mrs Merridew to go home at once. Her husband is waiting anxiously for her and prepared to forget the past if she will only come back. It is for this reason that I say no more about your conduct in this affair or about the consequences which will follow if Mrs Merridew does not return within four days.

Basil approved the letter.

'Try not to worry too much,' counselled Mr Mallet. 'I'll let you know if I have any reply, but I hope that you may hear something first.'

'You're very kind.'

A few days later Basil received a message asking him to call on Mr Mallet.

'I've had a reply,' said the solicitor. 'Not very satisfactory, I'm afraid.'

This is what Nicholas had written:

Dear Sir, Your client's effrontery does not surprise me. His wife has come to us of her own free will for protection. Nevertheless, in view of the threat implied in your letter and the fact that I do not wish to be involved in legal proceedings, I asked Mrs Merridew if she would return to your client. I am bound to say that I did so against the will of my wife and with a feeling of great reluctance. I felt ashamed of asking anyone to live with your client. I was not surprised when Mrs Merridew said that she would prefer to jump into the Thames and added that, if we turned her out, that is what she would do rather than return to your client. May I ask what you as an officer of the law would do in such a case? I believe Mrs Merridew to be desperate. If I turn her out she may commit suicide. If she did, would I not be a party to that crime? Would not your client? Would not you? In the light of these facts, do you and your client still request me to send Mrs Merridew home?

'The blackguard,' said Basil. 'A tissue of lies. We've never had a quarrel – not that you could speak of. As I told you, she was devoted to me until that little rat started to come between us. Well, what are we to do?'

'It's not easy. At the moment you've nothing but your own evidence, and I can only guess at what your wife and Drewe will say.' Mr Mallet thought for a moment. Then he said:

'I think our next course will be to write and ask if Mrs Merridew has any objection to being examined by a psychologist. If she objects, we'll have to think again. If she agrees, however, we should be able to find out whether she really is in the frame of mind Mr Drewe suggests. If their story is correct, she's terrified of living with you. A psychologist should be able to find out whether she really is. If your story's true, she isn't in the least afraid.'

'Of course my story's true.'

'Naturally, I accept your word, Mr Merridew. It isn't for me to try the case, but to do my best for you. Now, d'you agree to my suggestion?'

'I leave everything to you.'

The necessary letter was written and to Mr Mallet's surprise Mr Drewe replied that Mrs Merridew was quite prepared to be examined by a psychologist. In consequence, a few days later Dr Shrewsbury Cannon called at Nicholas's flat.

'I've come to see Mrs Merridew,' he said.

'Come in. She'll see you in here. Treat her gently, please, Doctor. We're very worried about her.'

'Of course.'

Shortly afterwards Elizabeth came into the room. 'Please go away,' she said to Nicholas and Petula. 'I'd like to see the doctor alone.' They went out. Elizabeth turned to the doctor.

'Hullo,' she said – but it was not just an ordinary 'hullo'.

There was everything in it which Elizabeth could put, and that was saying a good deal. The doctor began to wonder if he was wise to let Nicholas and Petula go away. However, he quickly recovered.

'Well – now,' he said. 'What's the trouble?'

'Trouble?' said Elizabeth, opening her large eyes. 'Trouble? Can't a woman leave her husband without being thought to be ill?'

'Would you mind telling me why you left him?'

'Are you a married man?'

'I am.'

'Well, I thought I wanted a change. Don't you ever?' and she looked at him.

'I don't feel called on to answer your questions,' said the doctor a little brusquely. He was extremely happily married but few men could have looked at Elizabeth, when she was really trying, without feeling the need of a little moral support.

'It looks as though I've been wasting my time,' he went on.

'It does,' said Elizabeth and looked at the ground.

Dr Shrewsbury Cannon's report to Mr Mallet was short: 'There is nothing whatever the matter with Mrs Merridew, except that she is very beautiful and knows it. She's not frightened of anyone.' He might fairly have added that, on the contrary, he had been a little frightened of her.

'Good news, as far as it goes,' said Mr Mallet, when Basil next called on him. 'The doctor entirely supports what you say. That, combined with Drewe's letter, gives us something to go upon. Why should he lie about her condition if he's got nothing to hide? On the other hand, from what the doctor told me on the phone – you don't mind my saying this, I hope – it would seem that your wife is more inclined to entice than be enticed.'

'That's just her little way,' said Basil. 'I've been very stupid, I know. I ought to have kicked him out months ago, but I couldn't believe there was anything wrong. Why shouldn't he give her presents? We've lived practically as one family for years. Now I come to think of it, though, the presents have gradually become of a more intimate kind, if you understand what I mean. Clever devil. He's always done it openly. Handbags, umbrellas, hats via nylons to other underclothes. I confess I did think it a bit odd when he brought home a brassière for her – but, even then, I couldn't suspect him or her. D'you know, I even made a joke about it, ass that I was. How they must have laughed.'

'You say "they".'

'Well – she's grown up, you know, and I can't pretend she's blameless, but she'd never have gone if Nicholas hadn't persuaded her.'

'What d'you suppose Mrs Drewe thinks about it?'

'Oh, they've drawn the wool over her eyes good and proper, no doubt. She's a complete nit-wit and adores Nicholas. She'll do anything he says and accept anything he does without question.'

'Well, it isn't going to be easy, but we have got some sort of a case to go on. Have you those letters you said you'd try to find?' These were letters which Elizabeth had written (or was supposed to have written) during temporary enforced separations.

'I've only been able to find one. It was written when I had to go North on business – only for a few days – about a year ago. Is that recent enough?'

'Better than nothing, anyway. Let me see.'

The letter began:

'My own darling tuppenny.'

'That refers to a rather stupid joke we had between us. I can explain it, if necessary.'

'Not at the moment. Let me read it all first.' Mr Mallet read on:

It seems ages since I last saw you (in point of fact it's only twenty-four hours, but in each one of these hours I've been thinking of nothing but you – or very little else – I've had to eat, of course). How is my own sweet pumpkin? His bed looks so terribly empty at night – and it is, too. I played tennis with Nicholas and Petula and a queer-looking man called Tramp or Cramp or something. He's an acquaintance of Nicholas. D'you know him? He never looks at you when he speaks, but sort of blinks at the ground and when he shakes hands with you it really is exactly like holding a limp rag. How he manages to use a tennis racket I just don't know. How is my sweetest sniffkin and when is he coming back to his own threehalfpenny?

'Well,' said Mr Mallet, 'that doesn't look as though you ill-treated her a year ago. Have you got the envelope to prove the date of posting?'

'I'm afraid not.'

'Well – never mind – it's her handwriting at all events and you haven't been away from each other so often, except in the war. All right, then. I'll write him one more letter and, if she doesn't come back, I'll issue a writ, if you agree.'

'I leave it entirely to you – but remember, most of all I want Elizabeth back – don't miss a chance of that – but, if I can't, then let's hit that swine for six.'

'I quite understand.'

'Now, about expenses. I can't afford a great deal. How much will it cost me all told?'

'That's difficult to say, but I'll keep the costs down as low as possible.'

Mr Mallet already saw some useful publicity for himself if the action came to trial, and he was quite prepared to take this into consideration in charging his client. It must, however, be said to his credit that in his conduct of the action he only had his client's interests at heart, and, should it have been better for him for the action to be settled out of Court, he would cheerfully have tried to arrange it. So Basil gave him £25 on account, and a further letter went to Nicholas.

'Your client,' replied Nicholas, 'can take a running jump at himself or you, whichever he prefers, and if you really want to serve a writ on me – which I doubt – I expect your client is bluffing as usual – like when he pretended to commit suicide – my solicitor will accept service on my behalf. His name is Theobald Gateshead and his address is 17 Birdston Street, Strand, WC.'

'Suicide,' said Basil with a fine show of indignation (a particularly good effort, in view of the fact that he had dictated the letter himself). 'Just another of his lies. I was trying to re-light the refrigerator – we have a gas one and it had gone out. I came home and the place smelled of gas. While I was on the ground trying to re-light it, Nicholas and Elizabeth came in. "Tired of life?" he said. As a matter of fact, it was just as well they did come in. I'd forgotten to get rid of the gas in the room and was just going to light the match. There might have been a nasty explosion. That's all there is to that episode.'

'Humph,' said Mr Mallet. 'Your friend Mr Drewe seems to be providing us with quite a bit of straw for our bricks. It's a pity we can't keep up this correspondence. We might get some more material. However, we've done quite nicely for a start. I'll issue the writ tomorrow.'

Nicholas had already engaged the services of another keen young solicitor – Mr Gateshead – and, after the writ had been received, he and Elizabeth and Petula had an interview with him.

'This will give you an idea of the sort of man he is,' said Elizabeth, and handed to Mr Gateshead a letter in Basil's handwriting:

You will do as I say, not just as you want. I'm getting a little tired of pretty Fanny's way. You say you didn't like the sherry. Well, you asked for it. And there's plenty more where that came from.

'That refers to a dinner we had at the Iron Duke.' This was a most exclusive London restaurant. The food was not particularly good there, but the decorations and prices were superb. With a few exceptions, only really rich or really unpleasant people went there.

'He threw a glass of sherry in her face and we all got turned out,' said Nicholas.

'D'you think we could get the manager to give evidence of that, if necessary?' asked Mr Gateshead.

'I don't see why not,' said Nicholas. 'I dare say he wouldn't like the publicity, but he can't have forgotten the incident. It happened very recently, and he himself showed us to the door. He wouldn't like to have to say that that sort of thing happened in his restaurant so often that he's forgotten it.'

'I'll go to see him,' said Mr Gateshead.

Mr Legotti had certainly not forgotten the incident. He had been appalled. The party had just ordered a particularly expensive dinner. They had banked on being turned out, as they could not possibly have paid for it. 'Caviare, turtle soup, lobster thermidor, and wild duck *à la presse*. We'll talk about a sweet or a savoury later.' Then came the sherry incident and the dinner was stillborn.

Elizabeth had complained that the sherry was too dry.

'It is not,' said Basil, loudly.

'But I do find it too dry,' complained Elizabeth.

'It is just right,' said Basil more loudly.

By this time the rich and unpleasant customers of Mr Legotti were all staring at their table, and Mr Legotti himself could not refrain from casting a glance in their direction.

'It really is too dry,' said Elizabeth.

'Well, see if this is less dry,' said Basil and threw the contents of his glass in her face.

At another interview Mr Gateshead asked Petula if she had seen any undue familiarity between Nicholas and Elizabeth.

'Well, you know how it is when people are so friendly as we all were. We all kiss each other, of course.'

'Just ordinary good night and so on?'

'And so on?'

'I mean similar kisses – good-bye, good morning and so forth.'

'Oh – yes, all those,' said Petula.

'Anything besides?'

Petula looked at Nicholas and Elizabeth. 'Well, there was just that once when I came home, you remember.'

Nicholas and Elizabeth shifted a little in their chairs.

'That was nothing,' they said. 'We told you so at the time,' added Nicholas.

'No, of course it was nothing,' said Petula, 'but the gentleman asked me and I've sworn to tell the truth.'

'Well, you haven't yet sworn, Mrs Drewe, but you're quite right to tell me the truth now. Much better than it coming out first time in the witness box. Now, I must ask you this. I'm sorry, but I must. Is there anything between you two?'

'Of course not,' said Petula. 'D'you think I'd allow it?'

Mr Gateshead was a little embarrassed. He was a young man and it was rather difficult for him. However, he stuck to his guns. 'I'd just like you both to confirm that – for formality's sake,' he added.

'You've heard what Mrs Drewe has said,' said Nicholas. 'Isn't that good enough for you?'

'Mr Gateshead thinks I'm a bad woman,' said Elizabeth, giving him one of her looks.

Precisely, thought Mr Gateshead, but out loud he said:'I

only want your denials. It's necessary for me as your lawyer to have them.'

'Just our denials?' asked Elizabeth.

'Yes.'

'Well, of course,' said Elizabeth. 'He has them, hasn't he, Nicholas?'

'I wouldn't be here if he hadn't,' said Nicholas, and Mr Gateshead felt he had to be satisfied with that. Just as they were leaving, Nicholas took Mr Gateshead on one side and asked to see him privately. An interview was accordingly arranged.

'Well,' said Mr Gateshead, 'I felt there was something I didn't know.'

'It's just this,' said Nicholas. 'This woman's becoming a confounded nuisance. I don't want her about the place.'

This was not what Mr Gateshead had expected.

'But my wife insists on letting her stay. I can't stand much more of it. What I want to know is, will it prejudice my case if I turn her out before it's heard?'

Mr Gateshead thought. 'That's not an easy question to answer at all. In some ways it might be a good thing, but it would certainly be said that it had only been done for the purposes of bolstering up your defence. Then, if your wife said that she didn't want her to go and it was you who made her, that might possibly prejudice your case. I don't know. I think it's one of those occasions where it's best to follow the maxim: When in doubt, don't. I should let her stay until the case is over.'

'Well, for heaven's sake, get it on as quickly as possible.'

'I'll do all I can.'

So the action proceeded at rather more than the usual speed, for both litigants and both solicitors were anxious to have it tried as soon as possible. Counsel had, of course, to be engaged on both sides. The solicitors were a little disappointed that their clients could not afford the services of fashionable silks. Indeed, it had been necessary to brief quite young counsel, having regard to the financial situation. For the Plaintiff was Mr G. U. Turnberry and for the Defendant Mr A. L. Malton. Mr Turnberry was aged thirty, Mr Malton rather younger. Each of them had only a small practice, neither of them knew very much law, and neither of them was at all expert at examining or cross-examining witnesses, though they were both certainly better in this respect than the distinguished and experienced Q.C.s depicted by the average playwright or film scenario writer. They were, of course, delighted at the publicity the case offered them.

Eventually the great day arrived and the trial began before Mr Justice Broad and a jury. Mr Turnberry started to open at some length, but he was in the middle of explaining to the jury somewhat pompously and not very accurately the meaning of enticement when the Judge interrupted.

'Don't make too heavy weather of this little case,' he said.

Mr Justice Broad did not care for the type of action and Mr Turnberry's opening was more than he could stand.

The spanner which he threw into Mr Turnberry's works was most effective for a time. Mr Turnberry blushed, stopped in the middle of a sentence, paused for a moment and said: 'If your Lordship pleases,' and then completely forgot what he'd been saying, where he was in his speech, what he had to say next – in fact, he forgot nearly everything except that he was standing on his feet that he had to find something to say, that he felt that everyone was laughing at him, and that he wasn't so keen on doing an enticement case after all.

'Yes, Mr Turnberry?' put in the Judge genially. 'Don't let me put you out of your stride.'

'If your Lordship pleases,' said Mr Turnberry miserably.

Somehow or other he got going again and eventually Basil went into the witness box. He gave his evidence quietly and

well and as a wronged man should. He made an excellent
impression during his examination-in-chief on Judge and
jury. When the Judge heard that misconduct was not alleged
and saw what a good fellow the Plaintiff seemed to be, he
somewhat revised his opinion about the action. Conse-
quently, when Mr Malton rose to cross-examine, the Plaintiff was doing well.

'I have to put it to you, Mr Merridew, that you have
treated your wife with great cruelty.'

'Never.'

'I suggest you have.'

'I haven't.'

'I put it you that you have.'

'How many times do you want him to deny it, Mr Malton?'

'If your Lordship pleases.'

'Put some instances to him – if there are any – if you wish.'

'Very good, my Lord.'

Mr Malton then proceeded to ask Basil about the sherry
incident. He worked it up quite dramatically by requesting
Mr Legotti to stand up in Court and asking Basil if he
recognized him. Having laid all the foundations, he put the
final question.

'Did you not throw your sherry in her face?'

'Well, yes and no,' said Basil. 'Most unfortunately, the
sherry went in her face.'

'Most unfortunate,' commented Mr Malton.

'I hadn't finished.'

'Not finished the sherry?' asked Mr Malton with a smile.

'My Lord,' said Basil, 'must I be treated like this? I have
been perfectly polite to counsel. I was in the middle of a
sentence which I want to finish and he starts making game
of me.'

'Finish your sentence, Mr Merridew. And Mr Malton,
you might reserve your comments for your speech to the jury.'

'What happened was this,' said Basil. 'I was just going to drink when the Defendant either deliberately or more probably by accident jarred my elbow and the wine went into my wife's face.'

'Were you not turned out of the restaurant?'

'Oh, yes. The proprietor refused to listen to any explanation.'

'It seems a very strange occurrence,' said the Judge.

'It has never happened before or since,' said Basil.

'Were you not talking very loud just before this occurred?' said Mr Malton.

'No more than usual. As a matter of fact, the Defendant had been having an argument with my wife about the sherry. She said it was too dry and he said it wasn't.'

'I suggest that was you.'

'Oh, no, it was the Defendant. I agreed with my wife.'

'Did you not say as you threw the sherry – '

'He says he didn't throw it, Mr Malton,' interrupted the Judge. 'You mustn't put that on him.'

'Did you not say as the sherry left the glass for your wife, "See if this is less dry"?'

'Nothing of the kind.'

'Did you say anything which could be mistaken for that?'

'Well, at this date your client would twist anything I said – like the suicide letter.'

'Suicide?' asked the Judge.

'Yes, my Lord. They wrote and said I tried to commit suicide. The truth of the matter was – '

'We'll come to that later, if necessary,' said the Judge. 'Stick to the sherry for the moment.'

'What about Mr Legotti?' went on counsel. 'Would he twist anything against you?'

'I'm sure not,' said Basil. 'But he was so excited that I wouldn't personally rely on his memory.'

'Did you say anything he could have mistaken for what I put to you?'

'Well,' said Basil, 'I did use the word "dry".'

'You said "dry"?' said the Judge.

'Yes, my Lord. I said something like – I can't remember the exact words – "I'm so sorry. I'll dry it up." Something like that.'

'Are you quite sure you said something of the kind?'

'Something like it – not the exact words, of course.'

'Very well, then. Now, will you kindly look at this letter. Is it in your handwriting?'

Mr Malton handed up to Basil the letter beginning 'You will do as I say.'

Basil looked at the letter and laughed. 'Oh – that. Surely my wife's told you about that.'

'What does the letter say?' asked the Judge.

It was read out in full.

'Well, what is your explanation of that, sir?' asked the Judge. It conveyed a very different impression of Basil from the one which the Judge had been forming up till then.

'It was a game we used to play, my Lord.'

'What sort of game?'

'A sort of consequences. I'm afraid we called it "rude letters". This one was written ages ago – several years before the sherry incident to which counsel has been referring.'

'I suggest to you that it was written a day or two after the sherry incident – well within the last six months?'

'Might I ask,' said Basil, 'if it is suggested that the letter was posted by me?'

'It certainly is.'

'What utter nonsense. Perhaps you'll produce the envelope.'

Mr Malton turned to Mr Gateshead and Mr Gateshead

turned to Elizabeth, and it was soon quite obvious that no envelope was going to be produced.

'Well,' said the Judge, 'have you the envelope?'

'Unfortunately, my client hasn't kept it, my Lord.'

'The reason you can't produce the envelope is because that letter was written by me when we were both sitting on the floor and handed by me to her,' said Basil. 'I'll explain the game if you want me to, but it was pretty stupid.'

'It sounds it,' said the Judge.

'Not half so stupid as trying to pretend it's a genuine letter, if I may say so, my Lord.'

'You may not. You are there to answer questions, not make comments.'

'I'm sorry, my Lord.'

'Now, Mr Merridew, do you say that you have always treated your wife with kindness?'

'I do.'

'Have you not pulled her round the room by her nose?'

'Yes, often.'

'You say you have – and often?' asked the Judge.

'Oh, yes, my Lord. That was another game.'

'It doesn't sound very funny.'

'I'm sure it doesn't, my Lord, but a good many married couples would look silly if they had to describe in Court all the games they played with each other.'

'You pulled her round the room by the nose?' repeated counsel.

'Certainly, and she pulled me round the room – but not by the nose?'

'By what, may I ask?'

'By my tongue, if you want to know. We didn't hurt each other, by the way. I cannot believe that my wife is genuinely instructing you that I've been cruel to her. Look at the letter I had from her not more than a year or so ago. That reads as though I knocked her about, doesn't it?'

'What letter?' asked the Judge.

'A letter I happen to have kept, my Lord,' said Basil. 'My solicitor has it.'

'Would it be convenient if the jury and I had it now, Mr Malton?' asked the Judge.

'Oh, certainly, my Lord,' said Mr Malton. He would have liked to say that it was highly inconvenient. The letter had been disclosed in the proceedings; he knew what was in it and that it would help Basil's case. However, he could only consent and the letter beginning 'My own darling tuppenny' was duly read out.

'I suggest to you,' said Mr Malton, 'that that letter was written before the war.'

'It was not. It was written when I was in Liverpool on business about a year ago.'

'Have you the envelope in which it came?'

'I didn't keep it. I only kept the letter by chance. I always destroyed my wife's letters when we were together again. I should destroy that one if your client would give her back to me.'

'Now, Mr Merridew,' said the Judge, 'don't be melodramatic. Your counsel will address the jury for you in due course.'

Mr Malton went on cross-examining Basil for some time, but made little headway. His best point was still Basil's letter. The story about a game took some believing. He returned to the point again and asked for a detailed explanation of the game. Basil gave one, but it didn't sound too convincing, although it wasn't altogether impossible. After Basil had given his evidence, Dr Shrewsbury Cannon was called. Nicholas's letter about Elizabeth being terrified of Basil had already been read to the jury. The doctor gave evidence in accordance with his report.

'Did she strike you as the sort of woman who would be easily persuaded to do something she did not want to do?' he was then asked.

'I don't know about that,' replied the doctor, 'but she gave me the impression that she was trying to persuade me to do something I did not want to do.'

'How long did the interview take?' asked Mr Malton, cross-examining.

'About five to ten minutes.'

'And do you really mean to say you could form the view that she wasn't in the least frightened or in a suicidal frame of mind in that short time?'

'In less than that. May I suggest to you that, if the lady gives evidence, you see how long it takes you to come to the same conclusion?'

'Now, Doctor, you mustn't cross-examine counsel.'

'I was only advising him, my Lord. I'm sorry.'

Shortly afterwards, the plaintiff's case was concluded. Mr Malton then addressed the jury and called Nicholas as his first witness. He gave his evidence quite well. He was asked, among other things, whether he really believed that Elizabeth was frightened of Basil.

'She told me she was,' he said. 'I saw no reason for disbelieving her. I actually heard her say that she would jump into the Thames if we sent her away. I can't prove whether she would have done so. My wife heard her say it too.'

He denied Basil's version of the sherry incident. He had certainly not jogged his arm either deliberately or accidentally. Yes, he had bought Elizabeth a brassière. He had been buying one for his wife and she had asked him to get one for Elizabeth at the same time. He stoutly denied that he had ever suggested to Elizabeth that she should leave Basil.

'I can assure you,' he said, 'that Mrs Merridew is not a person to do anything she doesn't want to do.'

'That may be,' said counsel, 'but even if she had the inclination to run away with you, it would not justify you in asking her to do so.'

'Well, really,' said Nicholas. 'First, she has not run away with me. She is living with me and my wife. Secondly, no one has said she had the slightest inclination to run away with me. Thirdly, I never asked her to do so. She came to me and my wife because she wanted to. It's possible she has exaggerated or even misstated the reasons for her doing so. But how was I or how was my wife to know that?'

He agreed that his last letter to Basil's solicitor was silly and offensive.

'I am often silly, I'm afraid. I am not often offensive, but I was annoyed at being threatened. I apologize.'

Questioned about the suicide incident, he said that Basil's explanation was a possible one, but he hadn't given it at the time.

'Oh – no,' he said. 'I remember now. After we'd got him into the drawing-room, he said we could tell the story he's just told if anyone happened to hear about it.'

'How could anyone get to hear of it?'

'I don't know but that's what he said.'

The second witness for the defence was Petula. She was asked by Nicholas's counsel confidently if she had seen any undue familiarity between Nicholas and Elizabeth.

'They always explained everything,' she said, a little to Mr Malton's dismay.

'Explained what?' said the Judge.

'Oh, you know the way things happen, my Lord,' said Petula.

'I do not,' said the Judge; 'least of all in this case. Pray tell the jury what there was to explain and how they explained it.'

'Oh, well, my Lord. I've a good husband, and if you have a good husband you trust him. And I'd trust Nicholas anywhere. Even when he was in the Middle East, my Lord, I'm quite sure – '

The Judge stopped her.

'Now, Mrs Drewe, please answer the question I have asked you, and don't run on about something else.'

'I'm sorry, my Lord. It's so difficult to remember everything.'

'First of all, what conduct required explanation?'

'Well, nothing really.'

'A moment ago you said they gave you satisfactory explanations. Explanations of what?'

'Well, my Lord, I once came in and found them kissing under the kitchen table.'

'What was their explanation?'

'It was a sort of game, my Lord.'

'Did you see how he was kissing her?'

'Oh, yes, my Lord, like one does kiss. You know, my Lord.'

The Judge paused. 'I don't think you intend to be impertinent,' he said, 'but in case you have any such temptation I should warn you now that the consequences will be very serious. Do you understand?'

'I'm only trying to answer your Lordship's questions. I've never given evidence before.'

Petula then proceeded to cry. 'I didn't want to come here,' she half sobbed.

'Would you like to sit down?' said the Judge.

'Yes, please, my Lord.'

'Very well, then. Now, compose yourself and answer the questions. I wanted to know the sort of kiss it was.'

'Well, my Lord, if I answer the question, perhaps you'll say I'm being impertinent, and if I don't, you'll say I must. What shall I do?'

'Answer the question, madam. You know quite well what is meant by being impertinent.'

'Well, my Lord, there are so many different kinds of kisses. There is the sort of kiss which – well – the sort of kiss – well, not the sort you'd give anyone in the witness box.'

'Madam, will you kindly behave yourself. You know the difference between an ordinary good-night kiss and a kiss of passion.'

'Oh, yes, my Lord,' said Petula, rather too eagerly.

'Well, which was this?'

'Well, it wasn't a good-night kiss, because it was in the afternoon, but I don't think it could have been a passionate kiss either.'

'Why not?'

'Such a silly position.'

'What did they say when you came in?'

'I think it was "Hullo".'

'Did they seem embarrassed?'

'I don't think so. They did mention that they thought I was back early. I was a little early, as a matter of fact. I'd gone to see a friend of mine who was just recovering from flu and when I got there – '

'Please, Mrs Drewe, it is quite sufficient to say you were back early.'

'I was back early, my Lord.'

'Did you see them kiss just the once or more than once?'

'D'you mean on that occasion?'

'Yes.'

'Well – it's very difficult to say whether a kiss is one long kiss or several short ones. One has to be doing it, you know, and then I suppose one wouldn't be counting. Let's call it a kiss and a half.'

'We won't call it anything, Mrs Drewe. We want to know what you saw.'

'Well – I just saw them kissing, my Lord. I hadn't got – '
And Petula stopped in the middle.

'You hadn't got what?'

'Well, my Lord, I stopped because you might have thought
it impertinent.'

In this rather unusual case, where the truth might be
expected to pop out all of a sudden and from an unexpected
quarter, the Judge felt he should risk the impertinence.

'You had better tell me. What hadn't you got?'

'A machine for measuring the kiss, my Lord.'

The Judge said nothing for a second. Then he said: 'This
is a Court of law, Mrs Drewe, and I shall not give you another
chance. You know quite well that that remark was intended
to be impertinent. No, it's no use snivelling. The waterworks
do not impress me.'

'Now, with regard to presents,' went on Mr Malton,
mercifully. 'What do you say about them?'

'What do I say about presents?' sniffed Petula.

'Yes.'

'Well, I like them.'

'Yes, yes. We all do. But what do you say about the presents
your husband gave Mrs Merridew?'

'They were very nice.'

'Did he give them with your approval?'

'Oh – yes, certainly.'

'And did he always get you one at the same time?'

'Oh – yes, I think so.'

'And does that include the underclothes – brassières and
so on?'

'He never got me a brassière.'

'He never bought you one?'

'No. I'm afraid I don't wear them, my Lord.'

'Then why should he buy one for Mrs Merridew?'

'She does, my Lord. If your Lordship will look at the two

of us, your Lordship will see that I have what they call a boyish figure, while Mrs Merridew – '

The Judge looked at the clock instead.

'I think we will adjourn for lunch now,' he said.

After the adjournment, Petula went back into the witness box. Mr Malton felt he had better finish off the brassière.

'Did you mind your husband getting Mrs Merridew a brassière?'

'Not at all.'

'Was there anything strange in his doing so?'

'Nothing whatever. He had bought us both belts.'

'That may be,' said the Judge, who was a bachelor, 'but a belt isn't a very intimate garment, like a brassière.'

'Not intimate, my Lord?'

The Judge should have been warned by the tone of Petula's answer, but, if he noticed it, he did not do so in time.

'I shouldn't have thought so.'

'Well,' said Petula, 'I'm sure your Lordship knows best, but it's the first thing I put on and the last thing I take off.'

'Oh,' said the Judge, 'you mean that sort of garment. I thought you meant an outside belt. Perhaps I'd better not ask any more questions.'

There was a Mrs Jones on the jury. She was a kind-hearted woman and she was sorry for the Judge. 'I could explain it all to your Lordship – ' she began.

'No, thank you, madam,' said the Judge firmly, and he kept fairly quiet for some time.

Nevertheless, Petula was asked a good many more questions both by Mr Malton and by Mr Turnberry. At one stage the latter asked her if she trusted her husband.

'Oh, absolutely,' she said.

'If you hadn't trusted him so implicitly, don't you think his behaviour with Mrs Merridew might have worried you a little?'

'Well, of course, every wife who doesn't trust her husband is worried the whole time he isn't with her. I wasn't worried even when he was in Cairo. He wrote me everything he did.'

'How do you know?'

'He said so.'

'Lucky Mr Drewe,' commented Mr Turnberry.

'I think so,' said Petula.

'I suppose nothing would make you suspicious of your husband?'

'I'm sure he's never given me cause to be.'

'You see him kissing under the table. It's a game?'

'Yes, that's right. I forget what they called it. I'm not sure that I asked them.'

'He buys her a brassière – that's just part of the service. I suppose if you'd seen them in bed together and they'd said it was a game, you'd have been satisfied?'

'You must think I'm young,' said Petula. 'I should have known what that meant.'

'That they were tired, I suppose,' said Mr Turnberry, and sat down.

The next witness for the defence was Elizabeth. She went gracefully into the witness box, and took the oath quietly and reverently. Then she looked the Judge full in the face. He returned her gaze. One of them had to give way in the end, but it was not Elizabeth, although the Judge tried very hard.

'Are you the wife of the Plaintiff?' asked Mr Malton.

'I'm afraid so.'

'Why did you leave him?'

'Oh – so many reasons, but chiefly, I suppose, because I was tired of him. You understand that, my Lord,' and she gave the Judge one of her looks.

'Don't ask me questions,' said the Judge.

'Oh, my Lord, I'm so very sorry.'

'Any other reason except that you were tired of him?'

'That covers so many things. I was tired of the way he said "Good morning".'

'Are you being serious, madam?' said the Judge.

Elizabeth looked Yes at him.

'Will you kindly answer the question?'

She looked Yes again and gave one of her low murmurs.

'Madam,' said the Judge, 'will you kindly say something which the shorthand writer can take down?'

'Oh, my Lord,' began Elizabeth. Whenever she said 'Oh, my Lord,' she spoke as though she were a member of an Eastern harem addressing her lord and master. The Judge found it very irritating, but he did not know quite what to do about it. The case was inclined to get out of hand, anyway, what with brassières and belts and games under the kitchen table.

'Oh, my Lord,' repeated Elizabeth, 'yes. And I got tired of the way he said "Good night", and the way he shaved, and the way he ate and the way he undressed and – oh, my Lord, shall I go on?'

'You were thoroughly tired of him?' said the Judge.

'Oh, my Lord, yes.'

'You needn't say "Oh, my Lord" each time you answer a question.'

What shall I call your Lordship? looked Elizabeth. She looked it so well that the Judge was about to tell her to behave herself when he realized she hadn't said anything. He felt he couldn't very well tell her not to look like that. She would say or look 'Like what?' and they wouldn't get anywhere.

'Just answer the questions.

'Did he ever ill-treat you?'

'Well, it depends what you mean by ill-treat. He never hit me or anything like that.'

'Then you never felt frightened of him.'

'Oh – no – not frightened.'

'Then you didn't threaten to throw yourself in the Thames?'

'Oh – yes, I did. You see – perhaps it was very wrong of me, but I wanted to stay with Nicholas – with Nicholas and Petula.' As she added 'Petula', Petula nodded brightly from the well of the Court.

'And I thought he – they – mightn't keep me unless I made up some kind of a story. Do you think me very wicked?'

'Don't ask me questions,' the Judge almost shouted.

'Did Mr Drewe do anything to make you leave your husband?'

'Did he do anything?'

'Yes.'

'Oh, my Lord,' said Elizabeth. 'I'm so sorry, my Lord,' she added, 'but it's a difficult question to answer. Did he do anything? He didn't say anything, if that's what you mean. He didn't ask me to leave.'

'What did he do then, if anything?'

'He just was Nicholas, I think. Looking at them down there, it doesn't seem possible that I should have made such a mistake.'

'Mistake?'

'In marrying my husband.'

'Have you not considered Mrs Drewe's feelings in the matter?'

'She's very understanding, my Lord.'

'I'm beginning to doubt it.'

'What is your relationship to Mr Drewe?'

'Friendly, my Lord, very friendly.'

'What were you doing under the table?'

'A sort of game, my Lord, rather a nice sort of a game.'

So the case went on and eventually the evidence was completed and counsel on each side addressed the jury. Finally, the Judge summed up. Among other things he said this:

'I am very glad to have your assistance, members of the jury, in this somewhat extraordinary case. I confess I should have the greatest difficulty in making up my own mind as to the truth of the matter. Fortunately I shall not have to do so. That will be your duty. You have to decide whether the plaintiff has proved to your satisfaction that the defendant has deliberately enticed his wife away from him. The fact that she was tired of him, if you believe that she was, did not entitle the defendant to take her away. On the other hand, if the wife left the husband entirely of her own free will and uninfluenced by any deliberate act of the defendant, this action must fail. There is at the moment, in my view, insufficient evidence of any misconduct between the wife and the defendant, but, even if you think that it had taken place, that would be no ground for finding in favour of the plaintiff by itself. The possibility of misconduct is only material as showing a motive for the defendant's enticing the wife away from the plaintiff.'

The Judge then reviewed the evidence, gave some directions on the question of damages and the jury retired. Poor Judge, poor jury. In the normal case the truth has a nasty habit of coming out, but in Merridew v. Drewe, Basil and Nicholas, with the assistance of their wives, had so arranged the evidence that it was a very difficult task to come to any conclusion at all. They did not in fact mind what view the jury took, and if the jury disagreed Basil would have found an excuse immediately for discontinuing the action so as to enable comment to be made in the Press. They had introduced into the case a large variety of subjects which many members of the public and all the popular newspapers love. There was a wealth of headlines from which editors or sub-editors could choose. Kisses and corsets, games under the kitchen table, the trusting wife, the beautiful next-door neighbour, they were all there and many other things besides.

Small wonder that all the parties concerned were approached outside the Court while the jury was considering its verdict. Elizabeth was the chief attraction, but Petula was a good second, and journalist after journalist made his approaches. Basil and Nicholas, too, as they had hoped, were also invited to provide a story.

'I have a picture of my wife in the bath,' said Basil. 'Quite decent, you know, but I'd throw it in for another £50.'

'Let me see it,' said the journalist.

The jury was a long time out.

'If the plaintiff hasn't proved his case, he fails,' said the foreman. 'That's what the Judge said.'

'There's something funny between those two,' said another. 'Can you believe that any man would get a brassière for a woman if he didn't want to put it on her?' He turned to Mrs Jones and added: 'I'm sorry, ma'am, but we've got to face the facts.'

'Body belts and nylons,' said another woman on the jury, 'I'd like to see my husband buying them for the next-door neighbour. He wouldn't do it twice.'

So they chatted away, now referring to the sherry incident, now to the kitchen table and so on. After two and a half hours, they were still not agreed.

'Well,' said the foreman, 'let's see if we can do a deal on the damages. I might be prepared to find for the plaintiff if the damages were small enough.'

'What about £50?' said another.

After a further half-hour's discussion, the jury finally agreed on awarding Basil £75 damages, and judgement was given to him for this sum with costs.

The parties and their wives were so taken up with the journalistic attack on them that there was only time for Basil and Nicholas to shake hands with their respective solicitors and to arrange to meet them another day. Basil called to see

Mr Mallet in the week following. He paid him his costs amounting to about £150 and then said: 'Don't take any steps to enforce the judgement, unless you hear from me. I have a feeling that this may have done the trick. I can't tell you why. Of course, if she comes back, that's all I want and I shan't pursue Nicholas for the £75 and the costs.'

'That's very generous of you,' said Mr Mallet. 'I don't see why he shouldn't pay your costs.'

'I don't suppose you would, being a lawyer,' said Basil, 'but all I want is my wife back, and if she comes back I shan't in the least grudge having spent £150 to get her back, and I shan't let her go again.'

So Basil and Mr Mallet parted company quite happily. After all, from the solicitor's point of view the case had been won, the costs paid, and the publicity plentiful and useful.

At about the same time Nicholas was seeing Mr Gateshead, and paying his costs, also about £150.

'It was bad luck,' said Mr Gateshead. 'Plainly what we call a compromise verdict.'

'Oh, I'm quite satisfied,' said Nicholas, 'and very grateful for all your help. Now, I can send her back again, can't I.'

'You can certainly send her away, but I don't know if she'll go back to her husband.'

'Stranger things have happened,' said Nicholas. 'I shall let him whistle for his £75 and the costs. Don't accept service of any more proceedings, please.'

'I expect he'll instruct the Sheriff to levy execution. What shall I say to his solicitors when they ask for payment?'

'Tell them to take the usual running jump or translate that into legal language if you prefer. "My client has no suggestion to offer," I suppose you'll say.'

'Very well, then, Mr Drewe. Is there anything further I can do for you?'

'No, thank you very much. You've no idea how much you've helped me.'

Nor had he.

The net result from the financial point of view was a profit of well over £2,000 to the plaintiff and the defendant and their wives. There was no spectacular news at the moment and the papers eagerly accepted almost anything they were able to sell. Nicholas and Elizabeth even posed for a photograph under the kitchen table for an extra £150. It was really quite an achievement and, when you come to think of it, no one was any the worse off. The Judge and jury would have had to try another case if they hadn't tried that one. So they lost nothing. Counsel and solicitors were not only paid their fees, but had some useful advertisement. So they gained. The newspapers got what they wanted and were very willing to pay the price asked. Those members of the public who liked reading about kisses and brassières and so on had their fill of entertainment. No one lost, some people gained, while the conspirators made over £2,000. It sounds very much like solving the insoluble and getting a quart out of a pint pot. So everyone was satisfied. The nearest approach to the discovery of the conspiracy – and it was still a long way off – was quite unknown to the four concerned in it, so that they had no uneasy moments. It happened when Mr Justice Broad was going to bed one night. His attention had been drawn to a few of the articles in the newspapers and, as he was turning over in his mind some of the details of the case, he had a sudden thought. However, it never went beyond his saying to himself 'I wonder' as he took off his cholera belt.

Chapter 3

THE GROPISTS

'I WANT you to look really expensive,' said Basil to Elizabeth. 'We're going out.'

'I am expensive,' replied Elizabeth. 'At least, I intend to be.'

'Well, unless this idea of mine is a success, you won't be much longer.'

'Are funds getting low again?'

'We've just enough to try this out.'

'What is it?'

'I'll tell you later.'

An hour afterwards Basil and Elizabeth were strolling in the West End of London. Basil could always tell if Elizabeth had really tried by the way people looked at her. If only men did so, she was a failure, but if women had to do so too it was all right. On this occasion she was a great success, once even causing a slight traffic jam when a very human policeman was unable to keep his eyes on his work.

'We are going to visit most of the art galleries in London.'

'What a bore. I've been to the National Gallery. At least, I think I have. It's that place in Trafalgar Square, isn't it? Mother took me there once.'

'No; I don't mean those galleries. We are going to the commercial galleries, where they sell pictures – or try to.'

'Whatever for? We don't want a picture. You haven't gone long-haired and artistic, have you? At any rate, not artistic?'

'We are all going artistic in a sort of a way – you, Nicholas, Petula, and I.'

'But how and why? I'm very happy as I am.'

'Why? In order to live. How? I'll explain in due course. In the meantime, I'll tell you what you have to do. We're going to visit the West End galleries every day for about a fortnight until they get to know us. We are prospective purchasers of pictures. Don't you say anything at all except "Yes" or "No". Leave the talking to me. But you'll have to look at the pictures as though you liked doing so.'

'For a whole fortnight? That's worse than going to a concert of chamber music. I can at least go to sleep there.'

'You like oysters and Chablis, don't you?'

'Oh, I didn't know they provided them. That's different.'

'They don't. I provide them, when I've got the money. And that's the object of this exercise. To make money. To begin with, we'll have to spend some. We're going to buy a picture in the end.'

'That seems an awful waste. I could do with five pounds for some stockings.'

'We're not going to spend five pounds.'

'What do they cost, then?'

'They vary. We shall probably spend about £300 or so.'

'£300? Have you gone mad? Just think what I could do with that.'

'Think what *I* could do with it. Nevertheless, it's all going into a picture. But not until they know us. Just when they're beginning to think that we're not serious buyers, we shall buy one. I'll tell you more later. Come on. In here. Pretend you're enjoying yourself. Think of the new clothes you'll get if this comes off.'

'Yes – perhaps – if, whenever I look at a picture, I can be thinking of a new hat or a new dress, I shall just be able to manage.'

They walked into the Samson Galleries, where an exhibition of French Impressionists was being held. There were not many people there, and one of the directors of this old-established gallery circled round them and decided to make an approach.

'Good afternoon.'

'Good afternoon,' said Basil. 'I like that one.'

'Ah – that's a beauty. It glows – doesn't it? Look at it from here.'

'Yes,' said Basil critically, 'very nice. Don't you like it, my dear?'

'Yes,' said Elizabeth with a new hat in mind.

'And you'll be surprised,' said the director, 'when I tell you how much it is.'

'Indeed? How much is it?'

'I'll tell you. You see, we only want to make our normal margin of profit. We picked it up cheaply and so we can sell it far below the market price. I'd like you to guess what it is first – if you don't mind.'

'Not much below £1,750,' said Basil.

Elizabeth took a quick look at him. When he had mentioned paying £300 she had thought it mad enough. But £1,750 for a picture. What possible enjoyment could be worth £1,750? A mink coat perhaps. But, even if you liked pictures, £1,750 would require a lot of looking before you had your money's worth. And, she thought, I can always look in the glass for nothing. Still, she knew Basil was after something and so she kept quiet.

'£900,' said the director.

Basil patted himself on the back. If he had said much more than double, he would have appeared too stupid, but twice the price being asked was just about right.

'Really,' said Basil. 'That's remarkable.'

'It is. Look how it glows.'

They watched it glowing for a few seconds. Then Basil walked right up to the picture, put on his glasses and examined it closely.

'The quality of the paint,' he said, admiringly. He had little idea of what it meant, but he knew it was the right thing to say.

'Lovely,' said the director. 'Much better than Defence Bonds,' he added.

'You're right,' said Basil. 'Pictures like that can't lose their value.'

'On the contrary, if you brought that back to us in a year or two, I expect we could show you a handsome profit.'

'But I couldn't do that,' said Basil. 'It's pictures I want, not profit.'

'Ah, but it's nice to know you've got the value there. Then, again, if you saw another one you wanted very badly and couldn't afford both, you might be able to exchange them and even have a holiday abroad with the difference.'

Elizabeth wanted to say that she would just like the holiday abroad without the trouble of having to buy a picture and find somewhere to hang it, put it up, take it down and sell it again, but she knew Basil was serious and so she controlled herself and thought hard about a pearl necklace.

'£900,' said Basil, as though reflecting. 'I wonder.'

'What use are Defence Bonds?' said the director. 'You can't look at them and, with the pound falling every day, a picture's a much safer investment.'

'I agree with you about that,' said Basil, 'but it's a question of which. I'd like to buy the lot – but there, I'm not a millionaire.' He made another close scrutiny of the picture. 'You're right,' he said. 'Really lovely,' and then, quite casually, he added: 'You don't happen to be giving an exhibition of the Gropists soon, do you? I can't really afford both and, at the moment, they've rather got me.'

'The – ?' asked the director.

'Gropists,' said Basil distinctly. 'You know.'

'Gropists?' repeated the director slowly, as he considered whether to admit his ignorance at once or whether to make an excuse and go to look them up. Perhaps they were like the Nabis, whom most writers mentioned by name without stating who or what they really were.

'Yes,' said Basil again. 'You know.'

At that moment, to the director's relief, an old customer of his came in and he was genuinely able to disengage himself in order to greet Mrs Grantley Wotherspoon.

'How very nice to see you again, Mrs Wotherspoon. I do hope you're so happy with the little Renoir.'

'Enchanted. Everybody admires it. It fills up that corner just like you said it would. It's a shame that Henry doesn't like pictures. He didn't even notice it. But all my friends simply adore it. And they're so envious.'

'I'm so glad. Have you just come in to have a look round. Or do you want to be tempted?'

'Please tempt me, Mr Macintosh. I shall adore giving in. You don't happen to have that Monet seascape still, I suppose?'

'Now, that's funny. I thought you might ask me that. D'you know, I've kept it in my office just in case you happened to come along.' As they walked to the office, Mr Macintosh suddenly remembered about the Gropists. 'I wonder,' he said, 'if you've ever heard of the Gropists. I've just been asked about them and it's stumped me.'

Mrs Wotherspoon was in the seventh heaven of delight – she would have been in the eighth if she had known the answer. Here was one of the acknowledged experts asking her a question, coming to her for knowledge. If only she could tell him. She thought for a moment.

'Aren't they,' she began, 'aren't they those people who –

who –' and then she made queer movements with her hands. She had had sufficient experience of art experts to give quite a creditable imitation of the antics in which they indulge when trying to say something for which no known words exist.

'I know them when I see them,' she added boldly, 'but they're a little difficult to explain.'

Mr Macintosh was glad that he had not confessed his ignorance to Basil. He knew, of course, that Mrs Wotherspoon probably hadn't the remotest idea of what the Gropists were and that it was most likely that she had never heard of them. On the other hand, however, she had been 'doing' art for some years now and she might have heard the word somewhere. He decided to look in one of his many works of reference – after he had sold the Monet to Mrs Wotherspoon.

'You're right,' he said. 'That's who they are. Thank you very much indeed. I know now. Thank you for saving me from making a fool of myself to a new customer.'

'Not at all,' said Mrs Wotherspoon, beaming. 'Not at all. You have always been so kind to me. I'm delighted to respond.'

As a matter of fact, over the years Mr Macintosh had been extremely kind to Mrs Wotherspoon. He had sold her many pictures and whatever he charged her, they always appreciated in value. If an impecunious person, in a fit of lunacy, decided to invest his last £500 in a picture, the chances are that tastes would change and a few years later it would not be worth half what he had paid for it. But with Mrs Wotherspoon, who was fabulously wealthy, pictures already worth much gold became worth even more. However much (within the limits open to a respectable art dealer) Mr Macintosh increased the price to Mrs Wotherspoon, the result was always the same.

'Here it is,' he said. 'Isn't that what you wanted? You

want it for your husband's study, I'm sure. I know just the place.' Indeed, he knew every wall in her large house and had been responsible for covering most of them. Only good taste had prevented him from making suggestions for one of the lavatories, which was more like a reading room. He had often thought what a good idea that would be, but he was not sure of Mrs Wotherspoon's reaction and it was not worth taking the risk.

While the Monet was being admired and shining or glowing or doing whatever a good picture ought to do – including, of course, being sold – Basil and Elizabeth completed their inspection and left for the Markwell Galleries.

'That was excellent,' said Basil, 'keep it up. I'll tell you what it's all about on the way home.'

Roughly the same performance was repeated to begin with at the Markwell Galleries, except that the manager there was a foreigner.

'Gropistes?' he said, with an accent on the second half of the word. 'Gropistes?' He looked really puzzled.

'Yes. You know,' said Basil.

He said it with such an air of assurance that even Mr Bronck hesitated, even Mr Bronck, who was not only conceited about his knowledge of art, but was fully justified in being so. He was one of the few dealers who could have told you (out of his head) what and who were the Nabis, what the name meant, how the group started, and all the rest of it. But Gropists, Gropists – who on earth were they? Eventually he made a decision.

'I have never heard of them,' he said.

'Really?' said Basil. 'It is Mr Bronck I'm speaking to, isn't it?'

'Yes, sir.'

'How much is that Sisley?' inquired Basil casually, and somewhat offensively changing the subject.

'It is not for sale,' said Mr Bronck a little curtly.

'What a pity,' said Basil, 'if it hadn't been too much, I should have liked it. But never mind, darling,' and he turned to Elizabeth, 'I believe they've one at the Rowntree Galleries.'

'Yes,' said Elizabeth.

By this time Mr Bronck's natural desire to sell his pictures had replaced his temporary but stronger desire to cut Basil's throat.

'I can show you another one which I think you'll like,' he said. 'Perhaps you'd be good enough to come with me.'

'That's very kind of you,' said Basil. They went into a small room and Mr Bronck produced the picture.

'It shines at you, doesn't it?' he said.

'Yes,' said Elizabeth, thinking of a new diamond ring.

'It looks as though it will be above my means,' said Basil. 'How much is it?'

Mr Bronck looked at the back of the picture.

'I can let you have it for £1,500,' he said.

'I was afraid of that,' said Basil. 'Too much. Very cheap for what it is, but more than I can manage.'

'It would be very easy to sell again,' said Mr Bronck, 'if you found you couldn't afford it. We often do that for customers.'

'Yes,' said Basil, 'but it's a picture I want. I'm sorry you've not heard of the Gropists,' he added. 'You will.'

Mr Bronck had now completely recovered his composure.

'Do tell me about them,' he said. 'I didn't think there was any group I didn't know. You mustn't think me vain, but I've had forty years' experience and I learned from my father, who was one of the greatest experts in Europe.'

'They're new,' said Basil; 'but I thought everyone had heard of them. I'm not an expert – not like you, anyway –

but you mark my words, they're coming along, like the Impressionists in 1874. They're cheap at the moment, but they won't be for long. You'll see. You'll be able to tell your son.'

'This is most interesting,' said Mr Bronck.

'I've not time to discuss them now,' said Basil, 'but if you can get me one' – he paused for a second – 'one with fingers or a whole hand, I'd pay up to £50 for it.'

'One with fingers?' said Mr Bronck, with some astonishment.

'Yes,' said Basil, 'or a whole hand. Now, we really must be going, darling. We'll come in again soon. Thank you so much. Good afternoon.'

'All right, all right,' said Basil to Elizabeth as they walked home. 'I'll tell you all about it. On second thoughts, I'll wait till we get home. Nicholas and Petula should be back by now, and I might as well tell you all at the same time.'

Nicholas and Petula had been spending a fortnight with a mad but wealthy aunt of Petula's. It was during their absence that Basil had begun operations, believing that the visit to Petula's aunt would produce no immediate result.

'Any luck?' he said when they were all together.

'The usual,' said Nicholas. 'Just before we left she called Petula into her bedroom. Tell them, Petula.'

'"I shall be dead soon," she said,' continued Petula.

'"You mustn't say such things," I said.

'"Why not indeed? Isn't it what everyone wants to know? I don't mean you, dear. You're the only one who's really fond of me and isn't after my money."

'I gulped something in reply.

'"But all the others. Riff-raff. I'm leaving everyone – what d'you think? – a whistle. All except you, I mean. You are different. I want you to have something to remember me by – something you'll really like, and then in the winter evenings long after I'm gone you'll be able to sit back and say: 'She wasn't such a bad old aunt after all.'"

'"Oh, auntie," I said. "I don't want anything."

'"It isn't much, my child," she went on. "Just your uncle's old travelling rug. Belonged to his father, I believe. I don't want it to leave the family."

'I ought to have been warned by the "winter evenings".

'"I know you don't want my money," she went on. "That's what I like about you. So I'm going to tell you what I'm going to do with it. No one else knows. It's all going for a fund to stop Mr Shaw's new alphabet. I think that would have amused him. It ought to keep a lot of people busy. All his money trying to build up something; all mine trying to knock it down. Good old Shaw. I liked his *Too True to be Good*, didn't you?"'

'She took me aside,' went on Nicholas, 'just before we left. "My boy," she said, "can you keep a secret?" I hadn't heard what she'd said to Petula, so I pricked up my ears. "I'm putting something in this purse, but you're not to say anything to Petula. I want you to get her something really nice from me when you get home. It's to be a surprise."'

'Ten shillings, I suppose,' said Basil.

'It was a cheque for £500, but in the place for the signature she'd just put "Whistle".'

'Oh, well,' said Basil. 'That only proves, as I'm always saying, that the only way to make money is to work for it. Now, listen to this. Let's all have a drink first.'

'You'll need it,' said Elizabeth. 'You don't know what I've been through.' She walked up to Petula, examined her face critically and said gravely: 'The quality of the paint.' Then she added: 'Don't worry. There's worse to come. Look at him. He glows. Come over here. You can see it better; the Defence Bonds don't get in the way.'

'What *is* all this?' said Nicholas.

'It started in a tea-shop,' began Basil. 'I've not mentioned it before, as I wanted to think about it first. It's a gamble, if you like, but it's worth it – I think so, anyway.'

'He shines,' said Elizabeth. 'Think of a pearl necklace, add a new hat, take away a picture and you're back where you started. He's been like this all this afternoon.'

'Patience,' said Basil. 'I was eating baked beans on toast. A man sat opposite me with a roll and a cup of cocoa. He appeared to look enviously at my baked beans.'

'I can't think why,' said Nicholas, 'unless he was very hungry.'

'As it turned out, he was – very. He had a beard and a certain amount of dirt, but nothing edible – except, of course, the roll. He made short work of that. At first his constant following of the baked beans into my mouth annoyed me. Then it began to fascinate. We watched each other. He watched my knife and fork preparing each mouthful and I watched him watching. I even played a few tricks with him, such as lifting up the loaded fork and then pretending it wasn't safe and putting it down again for rearrangement. All the time, of course, I was watching his eyes, as they moved with my fork. I felt a little like a snake-charmer. I believe I almost mesmerized him. Then, suddenly, I spoke. I just couldn't help it. I heard the words come out of my mouth.

'"Want a bit?" I said.

'"D'you mean that?" was the rather unexpected reply. I had no idea whether I meant it or not. You know what a passion I have for the truth. So I hesitated. Before I could answer, he went on.

'"I often get as far as this," he said, "but they don't mean it. They just laugh and go on eating. That makes it worse."

'"D'you mean to say that you're so hungry you want some of my baked beans on toast?" I said.

'"What's so surprising in that?" he answered. "You're eating them, presumably, for the same reason. I can't think of any other. I hate baked beans on toast, but at the moment I feel I could eat my grandmother – if she were alive, I mean," he added hastily.

'I pushed my plate across.

'"Finish the lot," I said, and, anticipating his question, "I mean it."

'"You're very kind," he said, and then was silent for a little – or fairly silent anyway. When he'd finished, except for a bean which had slipped into his beard on the way from the plate, he repeated his thanks.

'"That meant a lot to me."

'"I'm sorry you're in such a bad way. Have another," I said, and was just in time with "I mean it."

'After he had been supplied with a double portion, he looked happier.

'"This is how I get most of my meals," he said; "but it's an effort. You were fairly easy, and I'd like really to show you how grateful I am."

'"That's quite unnecessary," I said. "I know what it is to be down on one's luck. When you've made your fortune, you can send me a pair of silver candlesticks or a picture or something."

'"A picture, did you say?" he said, somewhat eagerly. "Are you fond of pictures?"

'"I wasn't serious," I said. "No. I'm not in the least fond of pictures. I don't even know what I like. Or rather I do. I don't like anything."

'"Then I'm afraid it's no use," he said. "That's all I shall ever be able to give you. I'm supposed to be an artist."

'"Really?"

'"I suppose the answer to that is 'Yes', but it depends what the definition of an artist is. If it means someone who

lives by art – well, the answer is 'Not really.' If it means someone who does nothing except paint with an occasional and
all too infrequent interval for eating, well then that's me –
really."

'"Can't you sell your pictures?"

'"I cannot. Look at this. Who'd want to buy this?" and
he bought out a roll of paper from some part of his clothes.

'"No – not that – sorry," he said and hastily put it back
again. "This is it, I think," and this time he brought out a
wider roll, which he proceeded to open.

'"Who'd want to buy that?" he repeated. I was about to
say "Well, why not paint something else?" when my eye
caught the picture and I was unable to say anything at all for
the moment. It was a picture of an ordinary wireless set and,
not very far from it, with no apparent connexion, was part of
a human form. Only part. It appeared to me to be a feminine
posterior. It was doing nothing in particular. Not that it
could.

'"I call it *Cable and Wireless*," he said.

'"Why Cable?" I asked.

'"Just to identify it," he said. "I expect you think it's
pretty silly."

'"I told you I'm not a judge of pictures, but I'm bound to
say that I don't quite follow what it means."

'"It represents," he said, "according to my uncontrollable
ideas, the spirit of the epoch. I have to do it."

'"I'm so sorry," I said. "Just think what a lot of other
things there are to do."

'He was not offended. "You're quite right. I ought to stop
it and become a grocer's assistant or something, but I can't.
I just have to go on. Shall I tell you how it began?"

'"Please do. But would you like some more beans?"

'"Just another cup of cocoa, thanks – oh, and, if you really
mean it, a piece of cake."

'"I was taken by my mother to the National Gallery," he began.'

'Perhaps I met him,' said Elizabeth, 'but I shouldn't remember. The only thing that comes back to me from that dreadful afternoon is the tea. I spilled it all over my new dress so that we should have to go home. I was rather fond of the dress, but it was worth it.'

'"I was taken by my mother to the National Gallery," he said,' went on Basil, '"and there we saw, among other pictures, the Rokeby Venus. Even you, little as you have seen of pictures, even you may have seen a reproduction of it. It's a picture of a lovely lady lying at full length looking in a mirror. For the most part, you only see the back view. The middle of the picture is taken up with her hindquarters. They were the part which caught my eye. I stared and stared at them. They fascinated me. No, more than that. As I looked at them, I could feel – I can feel now – an extraordinary sensation surging through me. I knew then, as I know now, that in some context or other I should have to go on painting them till I die. In the result, every picture I paint has to have them there. It makes no difference what the subject-matter is – a landscape, a seascape, a portrait – or even an (otherwise) abstract picture – there they always are. I just can't help it. What I'm seeking for I don't know – but I suppose it's my dream picture where they will fit in to perfection. As it is, they always seem to me to be just wrong."

'"I'm so sorry," I said.

'"You needn't laugh," he said, "I'm quite serious."

'"Then haven't you thought of fitting them on to a real person? That would appear to a stupid man like me the most suitable place."

'"You don't mean to a real person – they'd be most annoyed – just think what that lady over there would say if I tried – but you mean to a person in a picture. Of course I

have. But it just doesn't work. No – the nearest I've ever got
to it was my *Mill at Sunset*, but even that wasn't quite right."

'I was prepared to believe it, but I didn't say so. There
might have been a limit to his good temper.

'"Have you sold any of them?" I asked.

'"I thought I had once, but the lady was short-sighted,
and returned it next day in a fury and demanded her money
back. At least she didn't come herself. She sent her maid.
She was a nice girl and even offered to pose for me, but after
we'd had tea and so on there wasn't time."

'Then I had an idea. "This Rokeby Venus," I said, "she
has hands and feet and so forth, I suppose?"

'"Certainly. Everything you can see from behind."

'"Haven't you ever thought of doing another part of
her for a change – her neck, for instance, her arm or the
like?"

'He thought for a moment. "Come to think of it," he said,
"I never have, but I don't think it would do."

'"Worth trying, perhaps?"

'"If only I knew what I was seeking for. I'm in the dark –
groping in the dark – but all the time there's this uncontrollable force driving me on. I just have to do it."

'"Some more cocoa?" I said.

'"Just a cigarette, thank you, if you happen to be able to
spare" – he paused and I thought it was the end of the
sentence – but he went on after a short interval, "a packet",
he said.

'I gave him my last. I'm sure Nicholas would have done
the same.'

'Nicholas,' said Petula, 'would not have been there. An
instinctive reaction at the mention of the Rokeby Venus
would have told him it was time to leave. Am I right,
Nicholas?'

'Always, when we're together, my sweet.'

'Don't interrupt Basil, Nicholas,' said Elizabeth. 'He will be coming to the point any month now.'

Basil looked at his watch.

'I shall have to finish my introduction in about half an hour, as we have a visitor coming.'

'Now, he's not coming here, surely. You said he was dirty.'

'I am not referring to my artist friend, Mr Simon Plant, but to someone quite different and none other than Mr John Rock.'

'Not *the* John Rock.'

'Himself.'

'But what has he got to do with it?'

'If you will allow me to finish, you will learn.'

'I cannot see what a football pools expert can have to do with it. You're sure your lines aren't crossed.'

'Oh dear, oh dear,' said Basil, 'you are so impatient, all of you. I suppose you want me to start from the beginning.'

'Not that,' said Elizabeth.

'All right,' said Basil, 'I will. What is our object in life? Answer, to live happily. Can we live happily without money? No. Can we live happily if we have to work? No. Object, then, to make money without working. How have we done that in the past? By trading on human weaknesses. Malice and inquisitiveness have yielded good dividends, but they're not the only weaknesses by a long way. My present scheme is based on snobbery and greed. Is it plain so far?'

'Nothing is in the least plain. Suppose you get back to Mr Simon Plant and your last packet of cigarettes.'

'Very well. "Are any other artists like you?" I asked.

'"There are plenty who can't sell their pictures and don't get enough to eat, if that's what you mean."

'"But do any of them only paint one part of the body?"

'"Not that I know of."

'"I suppose they could do it to order," I said.

'"Most of them."

'"Of course, there's a good deal of character to be shown in a person's hands."

'"Certainly."

'"Or eyes."

'"Of course."

'"You happen to have chosen a part which is possibly less expressive than some others, but do you think you could get some of your friends to follow in your footsteps, but using another part of the body?"

'"As a commission, you mean?"

'"I do."

'"I expect I could. But what's the idea?"

'"It's only just occurred to me and I've only begun to work it out, but let me know where I can get hold of you and I think we may both hear of something to our advantage."

'"I haven't a card, but I'll write my name and address on the back of this if you like. You can have it," and he handed me *Cable and Wireless*. Here it is.'

'You're not putting that up here,' said Elizabeth, after one glance.

'Does he have a model for each picture?' asked Nicholas.

'He told me that he painted mostly from memory. Now, listen. This is my idea. It'll soon be summer. What does that mean?'

'A new dress,' said Elizabeth.

'Cricket,' said Nicholas.

'Warmer,' said Basil. 'It means no English football.'

Elizabeth and Petula exchanged glances. 'He's not been strange in any other way, has he?'

'No – just glowing and shining, you know.'

Nicholas had been thinking. Suddenly – 'I've got it,' he said. 'Picture pools.'

'Picture pools it is,' said Basil.

'Now, in order to start a pool we've got to get the interest
of the public. That isn't really very difficult if you go about it
the right way. We must get the Press interested. To do that,
we must stimulate in one way or another the interest of the
artistic profession, the dealers, the artists, and those members
of the public who look at pictures. It doesn't matter how
much we annoy them. In fact the more we annoy them the
better we shall do. When we've got them all talking, the rest
of the public will come in. Look how they flocked to see
Picasso. Half the people who went there had never been to a
picture gallery before. They heard about these new pictures
which were attacked by many, praised by a few and took a
lot of understanding. Of course, they didn't understand
them, but they went. Having got their interest in our new
group of artists – I'll tell you about them, if you haven't
guessed, in a moment – we then introduce the picture pools.
We take premises and hang, say, forty pictures. They will all
be of the new group. They are to be called "The Gropists".
Their founder is my friend Mr Simon Plant. We shall pay
starving artists a fee for hanging their pictures. Normally, it's
the other way round. We may even buy the first lot. Each
picture will contain some portion of the human anatomy and
anything else – much or little – the artist likes – except the
rest of the body. That would disqualify. These artists, led by
Mr Plant, are seeking for something – they don't quite know
what. As a matter of secondary interest, it will be pointed out
that the whole of the human form is really too much for one
artist. You can spend a lifetime perfecting arms, hands, or
eyes. That is what they are doing. One day we might have a
composite picture of a whole person painted by different
members of the Group. In exchange for an admission fee of
sixpence or a shilling, you will be given a coupon. This will
be arranged like a football pool coupon. For instance, on the
left (what you might call the home team) will appear Mr

Simon Plant's *Cable and Wireless* and on the right (the away team) Mr So-and-So's *Hands across the Sea*. Members of the public will be asked to record their opinion of each picture by giving it marks – say from one to ten. Of course, they won't in any way be compelled to record their opinions, but quite enough people will do so to enable us to work the pool. If *Cable and Wireless* gets altogether twenty marks and *Hands across the Sea* only nineteen, it's a home win and vice versa. If neither of them gets any marks (which I suspect may sometimes occur) it's a draw. See the idea?'

Nicholas nodded eagerly. He was already wondering how much the dividends on the treble chance pool would be likely to be. Even Elizabeth and Petula were beginning to see daylight.

'I see,' said Petula brightly. 'But mightn't it be difficult to run off with the money without being caught?'

'*We* shan't have to do it,' said Elizabeth. 'You and I can go abroad for a year or two while they're keeping out of the way of the police. I do hope you don't get caught, darling,' she added.

'We don't run off with the money, stupid,' said Nicholas. 'We shall be reputable pool promoters who quite legitimately stick to unnamed portions of the takings for expenses and services rendered and hand out the balance by way of dividends. Indeed, to begin with, we may hand it all back to get advertisement. Mightn't it be a good idea to declare all dividends to a unit of five shillings at first? That would swell the look of the first prize a bit.'

'We'll see how it goes,' said Basil. 'Now you understand why Mr Rock is coming here today. What he doesn't know about pools and permutations isn't worth knowing. We'll give him free advertisements of some of his systems on our coupons. The more permutations the better. The great thing is to get it started well. That's why we've got to run up and

down Bond Street and the neighbourhood plugging the
Gropists for all we're worth. It'll cost some money, but it's a
fair risk. D'you agree, Nicholas?'

'Yes; I think so.'

'Good. You'll be running it. Elizabeth and I will be doing
the advertising and shan't appear to have anything to do
with you.'

'How often will you have to change the pictures?'

'Oh – we can decide that too as we go along. The votes of
the public will be different each week. If there were a hot
favourite, it might be necessary to change it after a couple of
weeks or even after one week, but between you and me I
don't think there'll be very much between any of them.'

'There'll be nothing to stop people getting all their
friends to vote for a particular picture so as to help them
win.'

'Of course there won't. That's part of the idea. Just think
of the number of people coming in that will mean. And you
don't imagine only one person will think of that. No; provided we can get a really good start, we should make a fortune.'

'I'm glowing a bit myself at the thought of it,' said Elizabeth. 'We might even buy some Defence Bonds.'

'When I've seen Mr Rock, I'm going down to see Mr Plant
just to make sure everything is in line.'

Some time later that day Basil knocked at the door of
Simon Plant's studio.

'Come in, come in,' he said. 'I'm in a bit of a mess at the
moment. You see, I live here. But, thanks to you, I should be
expanding shortly. Yes,' he added as he noticed Basil looking
curiously round the room, 'I do a bit of sculpture too, but
I've nowhere to put them. I was going to say sit down, but
all the chairs seem to be occupied. Wait a moment. I'll move
this one for you.'

'Thank you,' said Basil. 'Now, how have you been getting on?'

'Famously,' said Mr Plant, 'thanks to your generous advance I have three full meals a day and paint very little. I shall come back to that, of course, but I've got to get used to the idea of eating again. It'll take a week or two.'

'Quite,' said Basil, 'don't hurry yourself. There are plenty of your things to go on with. Have you got that list?'

'I have. Here it is. What d'you think of it?' He handed a piece of paper to Basil. This is what it contained:

1.	Henry Crotchet	Hands
2.	Ernst Wasserbraun	Lips
3.	C. Y. Mandeville	Eyes
4.	George Goat	Hips
5.	Martin McGillicuddy	Finger-nails

'That's all at the moment, but I've promises from a dozen others. I held a meeting the other day. They were all in great spirits.'

After a short further discussion, Basil left Simon Plant, who was trying to make up his mind whether to submit for the first exhibition a small picture called *Drat that Fly* or a larger one, *Are you asleep dear?*

For the next few weeks Elizabeth and Basil were hard at work visiting art galleries while Nicholas and Petula, with the able assistance of Mr Rock, prepared the pools side of the exhibition. It did not take long before the Gropists were known – by name, at any rate – throughout the world of art dealers. In fact, the day after Basil's first visit to the Markwell Galleries Mr Bronck had called on Mr Macintosh.

'Some new nonsense, I expect,' said the latter.

'He offered me £50 for one with fingers or a whole hand. What on earth did he mean?'

A week later both these experts were surprised to find a

small paragraph in one of the newspapers which does not devote much space to art, referring to the Gropists by name. This happened to be a newspaper to which Mr Rock contributed, and the Editor, with whom he was on excellent terms, allowed him a few lines on the sports page, as the football season was nearly over. In fact, no reasonable request of Mr Rock would have been refused. He was the doyen of football pool experts and much beloved by the *Daily Sun*'s readers. It is amazing how far a few lines in a popular newspaper travel. On the day of the publication, Mr Sumpter Hedges, R.A., while happily correcting the proofs of his new book, was asked by his young daughter:

'Who are the Gropists, Father?'

Mr Hedges was a famous artist – famous alike for his excellent pictures and for his forthright opinions on modern art.

'Gropists, Gropists? Something to do with the Chartists perhaps. Look it up in a history book.'

'No; they're artists.'

Mr Hedges sat bolt upright, took his pipe out of his mouth and upset his glass of sherry. When order had been restored, he looked at the newspaper. This is what he read.

New Form of Art

Picasso caused a sensation and almost a riot with his pictures, but it looks as though the Gropists – the name given to a new art group containing, we believe, some of the more prominent modern artists – are likely to cause a traffic block when they hold their first exhibition in the near future.

The paragraph appeared just below the place where the dividends for the previous week's football pools were forecast. That was how Selina Hedges had happened to notice it. The journalistic 'we believe' can cover a multitude of errors. No prominent artist, modern or otherwise, was included in Mr Plant's band of brothers, but Mr Hedges at once assumed that one of the well-known artists whom he regularly attacked whenever he got the chance must be at the back of it.

'There he is again,' he said. 'If he could paint half as well as he advertises himself, he'd be in the top rank. If he could only advertise as well as he paints, he couldn't get a job selling bootlaces. Give me some more sherry, please, Selina. It makes me sick. I don't know what we're coming to.' He went back to his proofs, but he couldn't concentrate.

'Who on earth are they? What do they do?' he said. Selina could not help him, and, try as he would, he simply could not dismiss them with the contempt they unquestionably deserved. The fact that he had not seen one of their pictures (not even a reduced reproduction in black and white) made no difference. He knew he couldn't sleep until he'd confirmed his belief as to who was behind them and let off some more steam. He went to the telephone, and a minute or two later was talking to an old friend of his, also a great artist.

'Yes,' his friend was saying, 'Mary has just told me. She'd been doing her football pools or something and saw it. Can't make it out. Never heard of them.'

Mr Hedges toyed with the idea of ringing up his *bête noire* and sarcastically congratulating him on his publicity service, but he felt he couldn't take the risk in case it was someone else. He had a poor night. A few days later, in the correspondence columns of the *Daily Sun* appeared the following letter:

The Gropists

SIR, It was good of you in the face of so much blind prejudice against anything new to refer to the forthcoming exhibition of 'The Gropists'. May I venture to express the hope that your readers (and others) will look at our pictures before they pass judgement on them. I know that this idea is getting out of date, but it is certainly one of the formalities which even our group considers should be observed.

Yours faithfully,
SIMON PLANT

The handwriting was that of Mr Plant, but the wording was Basil's.

'Simon Plant,' said Mr Hedges. 'Simon Plant. Never heard of him. I know what it is. The blackguard. The coward. He's either using another name or he's just put up someone to take the first blows. Just like him. Can't face the music.' He went to the telephone directory. No Simon Plant. He telephoned several of his friends. No knowledge of Simon Plant. Shortly before the exhibition opened, an advertisement appeared in several newspapers in the following terms:

The Gropists

Five or six lunatics have joined together and exhibited their work. They take a piece of canvas, daub a few patches of colour at random, and sign the whole thing with their name. It is as if the inmates of Bedlam picked up stones and imagined they had found diamonds.

We shall be honoured if this sort of criticism is accorded to us. This is what was said of the famous Impressionists Monet, Pissarro, Morisot and others in 1876. Come and see for yourselves. If only we are as bad as they were. Exhibition opens at 10 a.m. on the 1st June at the Drewe Galleries, 11 Touchstone Street.

Special inducement: Every visitor will be given an opportunity of registering a protest against or recording his enjoyment of each picture, and OF MAKING A LARGE SUM OF MONEY.

'The police ought to stop this sort of thing,' said Mr Hedges. 'It's prostitution; that's what it is. Much worse than the poor creatures who get taken to Marlborough Street. They've no alternative.'

'Don't artists ever starve?' asked Selina innocently.

'Then they should give up being artists. Look at me. Did

I ever starve? Not a bit of it. Of course, I was hard up to begin with and it was a bit of a struggle – but that's not starvation. If you can't make an honest living at art, do something else at which you can.'

'Are you going to see them, Father?'

'No, thank you. I do not require a LARGE SUM OF MONEY. My means are sufficient for my requirements, and I am thankful to say I made them honestly and not by bribing people to come and look at my pictures.'

'But don't you want to see if there is anything worth seeing?'

'How can there be? Anyway, in the unlikely event of there being something worth seeing, I shall be told, and then I can go and see it. There won't be more than one. There won't be that.'

'Did they really say all that about Monet and Pissarro?'

'I'm sick and tired of hearing what was said in the eighteen-seventies. That's nearly eighty years ago.'

'But if prominent people made such bad mistakes then, couldn't the same happen again?'

'Of course people make mistakes and always will, but I can tell a good painting from pretentious nonsense.'

A fortnight later the exhibition opened. It was a huge success. Even the critics were a little cautious. Reminded in advance of the language used about the French Impressionists, they had to employ other phrases. Some, of course, dismissed the whole exhibition in a sentence:

'This is beyond criticism.'

'The only thing I noticed was the absence of onions.'

'The public behaved as though it were in an amusement park, but there was nothing to laugh about.'

Some critics, however, actually referred by name to a few of the pictures. For example, Mr Simon Plant's *In a Rectory Garden* was described as 'in rather bad taste', but *8 at Henley* by the same artist was referred to by another critic as showing 'splendid breadth of treatment'.

Within a short time it was plain that Basil was right. They were in the money. The printing presses rolled out pool coupons, the public voted for the pictures, filled in the coupons, bought postal orders, and waited for the results. The dividends rose steeply. The treble chance became the most valuable. It seemed as difficult to forecast a draw at pictures as at football. Mr Rock became as famous for his forecast of picture favourites as of winning football teams. 'Note Simon Plant's pictures,' he advised his readers. 'There is a type of person who always votes for them and they are therefore sure to secure some points. So never risk a draw with them. Keep the draws for the pictures you think will get no points at all. Here are my suggestions for this week.'

Walking into the Samson Galleries one day, Mrs Grantley Wotherspoon horrified Mr Macintosh by referring to the Gropists, but he was careful not to show his feelings and, on the contrary, he started to work out how much as an honest dealer, who valued his reputation, he could decently charge her for one of their productions. But £100 seemed to him like highway robbery. Yet anything else would probably make her refuse to buy it. It was an awkward predicament for him.

'D'you know,' confided Mrs Wotherspoon to him, 'I've been three times. It was so crowded I couldn't do it all at once. I wish they'd stop those silly pools. It brings such a lot of people there and many of them are rather undesirable, I'm afraid. I'm sure they think more of the pools than the pictures.' For once Mr Macintosh was inclined to agree with mob opinion, but he held his tongue.

'I don't mind telling you, Mr Macintosh, that I'm not at all sure they aren't the coming thing in art. What do you think?'

Mr Macintosh coughed slightly. 'I haven't had time to go there yet.'

Mrs Wotherspoon looked surprised. 'Not been there yet? But you must, you really must, if only for your own pleasure. I must own I want you to buy me one or two, but I'm really not urging you to go for that reason. It's so stimulating.'

'It sounds most interesting,' said Mr Macintosh, and realized sadly that he would have to go. He resigned himself to the inevitable. After all they wouldn't be the first monstrosities he had had to get for a customer.

'Have you any particular ones in mind, Mrs Wotherspoon? I was thinking of going there tomorrow, and I'd have a word with Mr Drewe.' He spoke of Nicholas as though he were an old acquaintance, although he had never seen or heard of him until the advertisement came out.

'Well, there are several, really. There's a most attractive little one of an eye. That's all it is. It's called *Going my way?* It's amazing what the artist has got into that one eye. You can see the whole scene. It's much more effective than if he'd painted all of it. So much is left to the imagination.'

Mr Macintosh commented to himself that the visitor could probably fill in the gaps better than the artist, but to Mrs Wotherspoon he simply repeated: 'Most interesting.'

'Of course, I know nothing really,' went on Mrs Wotherspoon, 'but it seems to me like an entirely new form of art. The more that is left to the beholder to do for himself, the better he likes it. It makes him a partner in the work, so to speak.'

Mr Macintosh would have liked to suggest that another good idea would be to exhibit blank canvasses and let the beholder do the lot, but again he refrained. He was, however, a little surprised at the fact that Mrs Wotherspoon was able to voice such criticisms. At any rate, they didn't sound too ridiculous. He did not know then that Mrs Wotherspoon had been well primed by Nicholas, who had warmed to the work.

'I expect you'll find them very expensive,' Mrs Wotherspoon went on. 'D'you know he didn't even hint at selling me one?'

'He?'

'Mr Drewe.'

'Oh, of course.'

'No, he just talked to me quite naturally and explained the partnership idea which I've mentioned and several other things which I've forgotten.'

'What other pictures took your fancy?'

'Well, there was another very clever one, I thought. Just two pairs of hands. One right way up, the other upside down. The first were obviously those of a jockey making a great effort to win a race, and below them was the other pair, a greedy pair waiting to collect the winnings. It was called *Past the Post*.'

Mr Macintosh reflected. 'I suppose there could be something in it,' he said to himself, 'if the drawing was good enough.'

'Any others?' he said aloud.

'There are so many really. D'you know, I'm almost thinking of letting you have the Monet back to make room for some of them, though I'd hate to part with it. Oh, there was a very grim one, but terribly good, I thought. It was just a forehead – obviously a judge's. It was called *And may the Lord have Mercy on your Soul*. I could see the whole thing: the prisoner in the dock, trembling with fear, the jurors looking away from the man they had sent to his death, the wife sobbing her heart out – all that and more, just from a forehead. You really must go, for your own sake.'

Mrs Wotherspoon had quite a good memory and Nicholas had spread himself for her benefit.

Eventually, Mr Hedges himself went to the exhibition. He chose a day and a time when it was least likely to be full. When he was handed the pool coupon, he looked blankly at the attendant who had presented it to him and said: 'And what is this?'

'The coupon, sir.'

'I've come to look at the pictures or whatever they are. What do I want with a coupon?'

'You never know your luck, sir. Might as well have a go. Cost you nothing.' Mr Hedges dropped the offending paper on the floor and moved away. His practised eye told him at once that there was nothing worth looking at, but, having gone there, he was determined that he should be able to say that he had seen them all. So he went right round the exhibition. He did stop for a moment at a pair of lips called *The Critic*. Subconsciously he must have realized that his own lips were at that precise moment very like those in the picture, set and determined and slightly curled, with no trace of kindness in them. He left that picture and passed quickly along the wall, not noticeably looking at Mr Plant's *What I think of the Critics*, which he almost brushed against on the way out.

'This must be stopped,' he said to himself.

An opportunity for a public protest presented itself to him not long afterwards. A dinner was being held in honour of an American artist hardly known in this country, though well-known in his own, but it had been thought, when it was learned that he was on a visit here, that such an occasion would be good for Anglo-American relations. It was one of those formal, yet informal, occasions; formal, inasmuch as there was a toastmaster and set speeches; informal, in that the speeches (or some of them) were to some extent improvised and punctuated by facetious remarks from the audience. The wine flowed freely and the speeches were correspondingly influenced. At last Mr Hedges had his turn. He was responding to the toast of British art.

'I am usually delighted,' he said, 'to respond to this toast, but I confess that today, for the first time, I am not happy about it.'

'You look happy enough,' said one of the even happier-looking diners. Mr Hedges glared at the interrupter and continued:

'I have always considered myself a progressive man. I hope I can say without conceit that I have done my best to encourage new artists, to foster the young idea and to examine without prejudice or preconceived notions every supposedly new aspect which may be put before us.'

'My hat,' came quite audibly from a corner of the room.

Mr Hedges affected not to hear this and went on:

'I am well aware that times change; I am well aware that standards alter, that new mediums may be found – '

'Media,' interjected someone.

'Gone spiritualist,' said another.

Mr Hedges turned on the interrupters. 'I hope,' he said, 'that I shall be listened to with the courtesy which I extend to others. It is perhaps symptomatic of this new world of ours that rudeness is mistaken for humour and that some young men consume more alcohol than they can conveniently carry. This was not so in the bad old days. But, as I was saying, there is always a firm basis for such genuine changes as occur. It may take some time before the new form is appreciated, but it has something about it which any unbiased observer can recognize even though he may disapprove. But just as one can recognize, without liking, the genuine new forms of art, so one can recognize, while loathing, the fraudulent forms which, decked in every kind of device designed to seduce the ill-informed public, try to foist themselves upon it. I have lived a long life – I do not say a useful one – it would ill become me to do so – but a long one – and I have seen many changes – '

'Not in the R.A.,' came a voice.

'Many changes,' Mr Hedges repeated, 'in every form and aspect of art. I have also seen spurious attempts at change – something designed to enrich the inventor at the expense of the public – something which the inventor well knows is no more art than, than – ' He paused for lack of a simile. It would not come. 'Which he knows is not art at all,' he went on. 'But never, never have I in my life seen anything such as is now to be seen – and heard, I may say – in this great city of ours. I am ashamed that our distinguished guest should arrive here at such a time. What will he think? What will he say about us when he goes home? Let me implore him to remember that these people who call themselves "Gropists" – I had preferred not to say the ugly word – these people, and those who for financial gain are backing them, are tricksters, mountebanks, thugs, gangsters, murderers of true art, and they can sue me for libel if they like. I should welcome it. I challenge them to do so. I brand them as a fraud upon the public, I say they should be in prison. My only regret is that this speech of mine is not going out over the air, so that all the world might hear the truth ring out loud and clear. I heard a whisper that the spoken word is slander, not libel; then let me say that in the book which I am writing and which will shortly be published – '

'How much?' came a voice.

'Too expensive for schoolboys,' went on Mr Hedges. 'In this book I will write down *verbatim* what I have said tonight, and we shall see if these creatures will have the temerity to take me to the Courts. Highwaymen and swindlers, cut-throats – '

At this stage the Chairman whispered something to Mr Hedges.

'I will not refrain,' he went on. 'Never did I expect a reproach from this quarter.'

'I only said you're repeating yourself,' whispered the Chairman.

'Apparently I need to do so, and let me say this before I sit down, that I shall go on repeating myself over and over again – no, not here – it's all right – until these criminals have been driven off the face of this lovely earth.'

He sat down amid tumults of applause, though there was some divergence of view as to what was being applauded – his forthrightness, his choice of language, the subject-matter of his speech or just his sitting down.

'Never heard him better,' said one.

'You'd have had to be pretty deaf not to,' said his neighbour.

But it is one thing when influenced by sherry, hock, champagne, port, and brandy to make bold speeches; it is quite another thing to make them good in the cold unfriendly light of next morning, as Mr Hedges was soon to find.

'When I was at school,' said Basil, shortly after the four had eagerly read a full report of the speech, 'there was a small boy who used to go up to bigger boys and say "Go on, hit me." He was eventually cured, so it can't have been Mr Hedges and, anyway, he's too old. Perhaps it was his son, though. It fits in.'

'He's certainly laid his head most artistically on the block,' said Nicholas. 'Even a fairly inexperienced executioner could hardly miss him. Pity we don't need the money.'

'*We* don't,' said Basil, 'but a lot of those artists could do with a bit. I rather fancy that most of Chelsea will go Gropist now, once the good news spreads that you only have to prove you're a member of the Group in order to get thumping damages. I'm almost sorry for poor old Hedges. However, we must steel our sympathetic hearts and resign ourselves to the inevitable. So must he. Go and issue writs on behalf of your-self and Petula and all the artists who've exhibited at our Show. That'll be about thirty or so. It'll do to begin with.'

A few days later Nicholas, armed with thirty-seven writs, called on Mr Hedges. 'No. I must see him personally,' he told the maid. After a short time Mr Hedges came out.

'What is it?' he said.

'Are you Mr Sumpter Hedges?'

'I am.'

'I have to serve you with these thirty-seven writs.'

'What on earth d'you mean? That sort of thing is done through solicitors.'

'Do you really imagine that solicitors would appear for cut-throats, thugs, and gangsters?'

'This is positively disgraceful.'

'My dear Mr Hedges,' said Nicholas, 'one of these days in the not too distant future you will wish you had treated me with the courtesy which, according to your speech, you normally extend to others.'

'Complete your business, sir, and leave this house.'

'At your service, sir,' said Nicholas, and added: 'With apologies for using the word "service".'

'Get out,' said Mr Hedges, and Nicholas went.

A few days later, however, in the offices of Messrs Rounce and Ponsonby, Mr Hedges began to regret some of the lan-guage he had used. It transpired that he could have been almost as offensive without rendering himself liable in damages, but, as it was, his persistent allegations of crime were (according to his solicitor, who was an old friend of his) likely to make his speech a very expensive one.

'Don't take it from me,' said Mr Rounce. 'We'll go to counsel if you want, but there's no doubt about it. You're on a very sticky wicket. Most of the plaintiffs are penniless artists. You're a successful one. Here you are trying to damn their careers from the start.'

'They've done that for themselves. The law's absurd. I refuse to pay a penny to any of them.'

'If that's your last word, well and good, but I can assure you that the only result will be that damages to the tune altogether of thousands of pounds will be awarded against you, and you'll be forced to pay. If that's what you want, there's no difficulty at all in getting it for you. You don't need my help. It'll come by itself. On the other hand, if, on consideration, you don't want to be ruined in that way, you'll have to eat very humble pie at once. It won't be easy or pleasant. After what you've said, I can understand your not wanting to retract. But there are no two ways about it. They'll make you pay quite a bit in any event – but if you withdraw and apologize handsomely at once, you'll get away with your life. Not otherwise. No doubt you'd like to think it over, or we'll go to counsel if you wish.'

'You seem to be on their side.'

'If by that you mean that I think they're in the right – well, I do. You can't call people fraudulent tricksters in this country unless they are. And just because you paint better than they do, you're not entitled to say they ought to be in prison.' Mr Rounce was quite as forthright as his client and, moreover, he knew what he was talking about. In the end, Mr Hedges authorized Mr Rounce to do the best he could for him. He found the plaintiffs uncommonly generous. £100 apiece and a very reasonable form of apology, which ran as follows:

Mr Sumpter Hedges deeply regrets that in the heat of the moment he said things about the Gropists and the organizers of their exhibition which he ought not to have said. He freely acknowledges that he has been treated by the people he slandered with great restraint and generosity and he desires publicly to withdraw and apologize for every allegation of bad faith which he made against them. He unreservedly acknowledges that there is no truth in any such assertion.

Nicholas had it framed and exhibited next to *The Critic*.

It must be said to the credit of Mr Hedges that thereafter he never said a word against the Gropists, and his friends tactfully avoided mentioning them in his presence. Although, however, he was effectively silenced, there were others to take his place. There was only one Sumpter Hedges, but there were plenty of other distinguished artists who were as angry and intolerant as he was, but able to exercise more self-control. It was in consequence of the activities of one of the more intelligent of these gentlemen that just before the Drewe Gallery closed one evening two officers from Scotland Yard in plain clothes presented themselves there. They requested and were granted a private interview with Nicholas. They told him who they were.

'What can I do for you, gentlemen?' said Nicholas politely.

'We've been sent by the Commissioner of Police to ask you some questions. The Commissioner has been considering with his legal advisers the matter of your competition. A question has arisen as to whether or not it is a lottery. The Commissioner has not made up his mind yet whether to prosecute or not and, in order to enable him to do so, I should be glad if you would give me some information. I should say at once that you need not do so if you do not wish, but naturally if you cooperate – '

Before he could finish the sentence, Nicholas interrupted.

'I must stop you, Inspector. Come and look at this before you say another word. It's too good to be true.'

He led the surprised inspector into the exhibition and up to a picture of a clenched and threatening fist. It was entitled: *You are not obliged to say anything unless you wish to do so.*

'How d'you like that, Inspector?'

'I don't like it at all,' said the inspector, 'and it is quite unjustifiable as a general comment. Mind you, I'm not saying that there aren't a few black sheep in the police who occasionally do things like that, but there are black sheep in every profession, even among artists and pool promoters, if you'll forgive me saying so.'

'Fair enough, Inspector. I'm glad you have a sense of humour. You'll like some of these pictures. Would you care to have a walk round. Just look at this one.'

He showed the inspector a picture of an open mouth. It was called *So I said . . .*

'The late George Belcher,' said Nicholas, 'couldn't have drawn a clearer picture of the scene. Look at that mouth. It obviously goes up and down all day almost automatically, stopping only for sleep, and even then it probably remains open. How d'you like this one?'

He showed him the picture of an ear. *Quick, under the bed*, it was called. 'Or this,' he went on and pointed at a picture of some pointed finger-nails with wicked sharp points. *Darling* was the title.

'Mr Drewe,' said the inspector, 'I find this very interesting and I'm glad you appear cooperative. At any rate, I shall be able to report to the Commissioner that this new art has some meaning.'

'Perhaps you paint yourself, Inspector?'

'Well, as a matter of fact, I do a little in my spare time. Nothing very much, you know. Just a hobby.'

'Why don't you submit something to us? I'm sure that with your experience you could produce something good. What about a couple of feet – *D'you know your car has been here for the last hour and a half?*'

'It's an idea,' said the inspector. 'Thank you very much. Now, if we may get down to business. Are you prepared to give me some figures?'

'Certainly.'

'What is your average weekly turnover?'

'Well – it's going up all the time. But last week it was £150,000.'

'How much of that is paid by people who never come to see the pictures?'

'Difficult to say, but a good deal.'

'Would you say more than half?'

'Oh yes, I should think so.'

The inspector paused for a moment. He had learned without difficulty all he had been sent to find out, but he didn't want to make this appear too obvious.

'You've made a remarkable success, Mr Drewe.'

'Yes, we have been lucky.'

'D'you sell many of the pictures?'

'Nearly all of them now. D'you want to buy one? I can let you have that one fairly cheap.' He pointed to two hands, obviously those of a surgeon, entitled *No swabs left in this time Sister?* 'I can let you have it for twenty-five guineas.'

'No, thank you,' said the inspector, 'but I hope you may be able to sell my pair of feet for as much.'

'I expect so. Perhaps your museum at the Yard would buy it.'

After a little further conversation, the inspector left.

A few weeks later Drewe's Galleries Ltd and Nicholas and Petula, the directors, were summoned for conducting a lottery and, in due course, the summons came on for hearing at Marlborough Street Magistrate's Court. The case made for the prosecution was that the bulk of the competitors had no opportunity for showing skill because they never saw the pictures.

'Most people who do football pools,' replied Nicholas, 'don't see any of the matches.'

'But they can read about them in the papers,' said the

magistrate. 'They can see the form of the teams and so forth.'

'You won't think me impertinent, I hope,' said Nicholas, 'but have you tried, your Worship? You can do as well with a pin.'

'I am not prepared to discuss football pool competitions, which are perfectly legal. You have to show me that there is some element of skill in your competition.'

'A large number of competitors see the pictures.'

'But only a minority.'

'The others can read about them in the Press.'

'Are there reproductions of the pictures in the papers?'

'No, but they're referred to by name and description in some papers. As a matter of fact, they're almost as amusing to describe as to see.'

'Not a great compliment to the artists.'

'I only said amusing. Naturally, the artistic work has to be seen to be appreciated. But the competitor who doesn't see them can exercise his judgement as to what will amuse the public most. For instance, sitting in this Court this morning, an idea came to me which I shall give to one of my artists. A picture of a nose with pince-nez on it entitled *Forty shillings*.'

'I see your point,' said the magistrate. 'I don't think this is at all an easy matter and I shall reserve my decision. You will be notified of the date when I shall give it.'

'Well,' said Basil that afternoon, 'if the worst comes to the worst, we shan't have done so badly. I wonder one of the big pool promoters hasn't tried to buy us out. We might make a serious inroad on football pools when the season starts.'

At that moment there was a knock on the door. It was a stranger. 'My name is Vulgan. I want to see Mr Drewe.'

'Come in,' said Basil, 'we've been expecting you.'

'Expecting me?' said Mr Vulgan. 'How is that? I never wrote or telephoned.'

'You are Vulgan's Pools, I presume?'

'I am.'

'I was just saying that we expected you to come and buy us out.'

'I see. Well, I shouldn't have come if you hadn't been prosecuted. You'd have wanted too much.'

'Well,' said Nicholas, 'what's your suggestion?'

'You may get closed up and you may not. If you lose, you're finished; if you win, you seem on the way to a fortune. Why not lay it off. Sell it lock, stock, and barrel to me for a reasonable price. Even if you win, the case may go higher. Keep out of litigation, I say. What about £50,000?'

'A hundred,' said Basil.

'Seventy-five.'

'A hundred.'

'You won't be worth anything if you lose.'

'You'll be worth a lot less if we win.'

'Eighty.'

'A hundred.'

'You're very obstinate.'

'We can afford to be. If we're wound up, it's just too bad. We've done quite nicely so far and can take the risk unless you give us what we ask.'

'You're not Mr Drewe, are you? This other gentleman is the one whose picture I've seen in the papers.'

'That's right. But we're all interested together. I'm more or less a sleeping partner.'

'Ninety, then.'

Basil looked at Nicholas. 'All right,' he said, 'ninety-five it is.'

'Done,' said Mr Vulgan. 'Now let's get down to details. What I want at once are the names and addresses of your clients. I've got the coupons all printed.'

'But you don't know our next week's pictures.'

'Pictures? Pictures? What d'you take me for? I'm not running pictures. Whatever the result of your case, pictures are no good. They wouldn't last. No, I'm starting something really good – something that will just suit the public – and no risk of it being called a lottery.'

'May we ask what?'

'You certainly may. Basutoland hockey matches.'

As soon as the deal had been concluded, Mr Vulgan communicated with the solicitors for the Commissioner of Police and, as a result of what he said, a conference was held between them and Mr Vulgan's solicitors. It was finally agreed that, on Mr Vulgan's undertaking to give up the picture pool, the magistrate should be asked to allow the prosecution to be withdrawn without giving a decision. From the Commissioner's point of view an acquittal might have resulted in a flood of fraudulent picture pools, while a conviction was unnecessary in view of Mr Vulgan's undertaking. The magistrate was quite relieved at not being called upon to give a decision, and he saw no reason why he should do so in the public interest. The prosecution was accordingly withdrawn by leave. Nicholas distributed a substantial quantity of the net profits of the enterprise among the artists who had contributed pictures, Mr Simon Plant getting, of course, the biggest share.

A few weeks afterwards Basil and Elizabeth walked into the Markwell Galleries. Elizabeth had a new hat, a new dress, and a real pearl necklace. Mr Bronck greeted them.

'I think I have what you want,' he said.

'Oh,' said Basil, 'how did you guess?'

'You told me. Some fingers or a whole hand, wasn't it? Look at this.' He produced in triumph a Gropist picture of a single finger called *This way*. 'There was another called *Get out*, but I thought you might prefer this one. Only thirty guineas. They're worth much more now.'

'On the whole,' said Basil, 'I think I'd prefer a Monet or a Pissarro if you happen to have one.'

Mr Bronck started. 'But they're terribly expensive, sir,' he said.

'So I believe,' said Basil, 'but this time I've come to put money into pictures. I've sold some Defence Bonds and want to reinvest.'

Mr Bronck was delighted and assisted Basil to invest some £5,000. They spent quite an enjoyable afternoon. Even Elizabeth enjoyed herself looking at the women who hadn't pearl necklaces. Just before they left, Mr Bronck referred again to the Gropists.

'I wonder,' he said, 'what was the origin of their sensational success.'

'I believe,' said Basil, 'it was baked beans on toast. Thank you so much. Good afternoon.'

Mr Bronck, almost in tears, telephoned his bankers and arranged to have Basil's cheque specially cleared. He was surprised to find that it was met.

Chapter 4

QUARTET IN THREE MOVEMENTS

FOR a long time after the successful conclusion of the Gropist episode the happy quartet played and played. They sampled every kind of legitimate pleasure. They had achieved their ambition; they had enough capital to last them the rest of their lives and they had for ever laid the hideous spectre of work. Not by incantations or prayers but by a skilful shaking of the trees on which other people's money grew. They stored away enough of the fruit for the future and proceeded to eat as much as they liked in every kind of place and always in perfect comfort. It was a type of existence for which so many people hope and pray each week as they seal up, stamp, and post the little envelopes which make pool promoters very rich. 'If only –' they say to themselves. 'Perhaps next week.' And they picture the mayor presenting them with a cheque in the presence of the representative of Grandmaster's Pools. Perhaps they will appear in 'In Town Tonight'. The eager imagination of at least one competitor pictures something like this:

'And now we have in the studio someone in whose shoes you would all like to be – or should I say in whose dress – very becoming, if I may say so, Mrs Sparke, I beg your pardon – Mrs Sharples . . . Now, Mrs Sharples, and what does it feel like to win £75,000?'

'I don't really know yet. I have never done it before.'

'No, of course not. What d'you think of doing with your great good fortune? Are you going on working?'

'I might do.'

'Not made up your mind. Very natural. But tell us something which I'm sure listeners want to hear: what's the first thing you're going to get? I'm sure each week people think what they're going to buy if they're lucky, and now here you are, the lucky one – what's it going to be . . . a fur coat, a car or . . . ?'

'Well, I think I shall get a wireless licence first.'

'You'd better not say that too loud. The Postmaster-General may be listening.'

'But we haven't got a wireless yet – that's the next thing I'll get.'

'Not got a wireless set? Good gracious. That must be almost unique. Then you didn't hear the football results on the wireless?'

'Oh yes I did – at a friend's. You see, my husband doesn't hold with the wireless. He says it makes a noise.'

'Surely it's only other people's wirelesses that make a noise, Mrs Sparke – I'm so sorry – Sharples. I shall forget my own name next. Anyway, that's the first thing you're going to buy – a wireless set. You don't think your husband will mind now?'

'He won't have to. As a matter of fact, that reminds me of the next thing I will get.'

'Ah – what's that?'

'A separation.'

The lady imagines a good deal more of the interview, but she would be wrong. As soon as the interviewer realized she meant what she was saying he would swiftly and even unceremoniously get on to the next item – the man who had been walking continuously for a month, day and night.

'You can hear him. He's even marking time in the studio. Tell me, Mr Turner, what makes you do this?'

'Oh, I dunno.'

Then there is the other type of competitor who has put a cross in the correct place on the coupon, and who creeps away, almost unknown, with the £75,000 and counts it over and over again, has a holiday, buys a business, loses some money, has another holiday, quarrels with his wife, buys another business, loses the rest of his money and starts going in for football pools again. Join the happy circle.

Basil and Nicholas and their wives did not fall into either of these categories. They deliberately and carefully set out in pursuit of enjoyment and they usually found it. But it could not go on for ever. Minds like those of Basil and Nicholas required from time to time something more stimulating than mere enjoyment. One day, while at the Riviera, they were all sitting together having a drink before lunch when Basil spoke:

'Here I am,' he said, 'with a lovely wife, two cheerful and delightful friends, as many acquaintances as I choose to buy – and yet I'm not satisfied.'

'Surely,' said Elizabeth, 'you're not suggesting you want two lovely wives and four cheerful and delightful friends?'

'I quite agree, old man,' said Nicholas, ignoring Elizabeth's flippancy. 'I feel just the same.'

'Thank you,' said Petula. 'I like that. Did you hear it too?' And she turned to Elizabeth.

'Dear Petula,' said Elizabeth, stretching herself gently and, as it were, unfolding her incredible beauty for the three of them to admire. Well as they knew her they could not avoid doing so, nor did they wish to. As Basil had said more than once: 'If you like pictures, you don't get tired of looking at a lovely picture even if you've had it all your life. If the picture happens to be alive, that should make it better, not worse.'

'Dear Petula,' repeated Elizabeth, 'you're pretty as a picture. I've often seen men looking at you in the streets.'

'Stop it, girls,' said Basil. 'I'm serious. After lunch I shall go to the Casino to risk £20,000. If we lose it it should make us think a bit, and we ought to get a momentary thrill watching it go.'

'Suppose we win?'

'Oh, we won't. But if we do we shall have to bear it manfully. While we're there the girls can go and buy something expensive. Then they can sell it again, if necessary, afterwards.'

Later that day they met again and Basil had to announce the doleful news that once more they had won. Good luck had dogged them wherever they went. They had started at the Casino in quite a small way, and now they had made another fortune. They were not even robbed in the street, and though there was a hotel thief staying at their hotel he never even tried their rooms. Very foolishly and quite falsely, Basil, while having a drink with him at the bar, had mentioned that he always left a tame poisonous snake in the sitting-room when they went to bed.

After announcing the news, Basil said:

'Tonight we shall drink too much. Tomorrow we must make a plan. If we go on like this I shall become irritable before my time.'

The next morning they decided to go back to London, and the day after their arrival home Nicholas and Basil had a serious talk together.

'Suppose we buy a racehorse or two? That might be fun,' suggested Nicholas.

'We could try,' said Basil, 'but it's not one of your brighter ideas. I bet it wins.'

It did. They tried backing it, but it still won. The final fiasco came when they won the Derby with a horse which all the authorities on racing said was incapable of doing so because of its breeding. It is true that two horses which were well clear of it in the straight collided and the girths of the favourite broke when it would otherwise have won, but accidents will happen, and Elizabeth, almost in tears, had to lead the winner in. She did not fully understand what all the fuss was about—it seemed to her very pleasant to win the Derby and to be photographed patting her horse's head (provided it didn't bite her) – but she realized that all this success was making Basil miserable. She was devoted to him, as was Petula to Nicholas; and as they had shared the sorrows of poverty in the past, so now they shared the misery of success.

A few days after the Derby, the quartet were sitting unhappily in the grill room of an expensive hotel just managing to get through a little caviare and champagne. Suddenly Nicholas put his glass down.

'I've got it,' he said. 'I wonder why it's never occurred to us before.'

They all took a quick drink and waited.

'Finish that stuff up first,' he said. 'I want your undivided attention.'

The caviare immediately began to taste a little better; they raised the champagne to their lips in a perceptibly more cheerful manner.

'Now,' said Nicholas.

Immediately a waiter came to clear the plates, preparatory to serving the next course.

'Don't interrupt us for the next ten minutes, please,' said Basil.

'But the chicken pancake is just made,' exclaimed the waiter. 'If it is left it will – '

'Unmake it,' said Basil. 'Put it in the pig bucket, or much the same thing, serve it to those gentlemen over there – but go away, please. Well, Nicholas?'

'Now don't jump down my throat at once. It's a very simple suggestion.'

'All the best plans are simple.'

'Well, it's just this. We've got more money than we know what to do with. Why not do some good with it?'

No one spoke. Then Basil drank some more champagne. He still said nothing. Eventually Petula could stand the silence no longer.

'Isn't that what we've been doing?' she said. 'I thought you were tired of it.'

'Good to other people,' explained Nicholas gently.

'Oh,' said Petula.

Elizabeth assumed her puzzled look to such an extent that nearly all the men who could see her wanted to kiss it and make it better.

'Good?' said Basil. 'It's an idea. I must think.'

He remained thinking for fully a minute.

Then, 'It's worth trying,' he said. 'Not at all a bad notion. Had you anything particular in mind?'

'I hadn't, as a matter of fact. It only came to me a short time ago. I was getting a flower for Petula. The girl I got it from was so pretty that I gave her a pound. It was the look she gave me that started me off. We're used to over-tipping, of course. But the normal look on head-waiters' faces when you give them twice as much as anyone else and ten times as much as the service they've rendered you is worth has never much attracted me. There's pleasure in it, to be sure, but mixed up with so much oiliness, sycophancy, and contempt that I prefer the man who takes it as though I'd undertipped him. But this girl, she just looked at me and smiled – such a lovely open happy smile – '

'Look here,' said Petula. 'Who were you doing good to?'

'No need to be jealous,' went on Nicholas. 'I didn't even get her address.'

'You know where to find her.'

'Let him get on, Petula,' said Basil. 'He hasn't finished yet.'

'That's what I was afraid of,' said Petula.

'She looked so intensely happy and pleased that I really got a kick out of it. D'you know, in a flash I visualized the wicked landlord about to turn her and her aged mother into the street – '

'A pound wouldn't go far,' interrupted Basil; 'and, anyway, there aren't any wicked landlords any more. They aren't allowed to be. All the new fairy stories will start the other way round: there once was a wicked tenant who never paid the rent to his poor old landlord who had nothing else to live on. One day a stranger came to the tenant and said: "Kind sir, will you give me ninepence for fourpence?" "Like hell," said the tenant. "Hop it." Then the stranger went to the old landlord who had only ninepence left to live on and asked him the same question. "Give you ninepence for fourpence?" repeated the old landlord. "I've been doing nothing else for years. I might as well."'

'Well – I thought a pound wouldn't go far either, so I made it a fiver. And then she – '

'I don't want to hear any more,' said Petula. 'No, I'm sure it's perfectly all right and above board, but I just prefer not to know.'

'Petula,' said Basil, 'you must keep quiet. You know perfectly well that if Nicholas is ever guilty of the slightest impropriety – and I'm sure he isn't – he does it most discreetly and lies to you like a trooper if you suspect anything. Go on, Nicholas.'

'She just looked at me and said, "It must be great fun being able to make people happy so simply."'

'What did you say?'

'I treated it all very lightly. I just said "How d'you know it's simple? It might have been my last fiver and I might be just about to throw myself in the Thames."'

'"That's quite simple, too," she said. "That's the great

thing about life. You can always get rid of it if you don't like it. But I'm sure it isn't that in your case. I can see by your face that you're kind. You just love making people happy."

"I'm glad I've made you happy," I said – '

'Don't you think I might have something to eat?' said Petula. 'I should find the tale of Nicholas and the beautiful flower girl easier to stomach if I could get my teeth into something – preferably some raw meat.'

'It's all over,' said Nicholas. 'That's all there is to it. But it really did give me such a thrill to see that girl's face – it lighted up so – it – '

'All right,' said Basil. 'We've got your point. You needn't elaborate for Petula's benefit. She's been keeping up with us this time.'

'A bit ahead, I should say,' said Elizabeth.

'Well,' said Basil, 'admittedly it's a novel idea, but personally I'm all in favour of something new. Mark you, we may just make fools of ourselves and, when it comes to it, we may not like it at all. Everyone isn't like Nicholas's flower girl – and she probably didn't need any help whatsoever. However, I think that the best thing will be if we try it out gradually, then if it seems to work, we can go in for it in a big way. I'll make a recce tomorrow. I'll call at the Vicarage and give the old boy £2,000 for something and see what it feels like. That'll be a fair test. I'm not impugning Nicholas's good faith, but the flower girl wasn't. D'you all agree?'

The proposal was carried and next morning Basil found out the name of the Vicar, telephoned him, and made an appointment for the following day.

The Reverend Matthew Pudsey had not always been a parson. He had been in business, a solicitor, and a school-master. Each time, however, he had failed because, to make a success, he would have had to have done things quite alien to his nature. In business he insisted on reading all the official

forms he had to sign before signing them, and he refused to
sign any statement which was not wholly accurate or to make
any promise which he had not some reasonable expectation
of being able to fulfil. His business associates soon tired of
this. 'We'll go bust if you spend all your time like that,' they
said. 'Everyone signs these things. There's nothing to it. The
Ministry doesn't expect you to keep your word.'

'Then the Ministry shouldn't ask me to sign,' he would
say. Sometimes he altered a form so as to make his declara-
tion accurate. No Government department can tolerate this.
Either you sign the printed form unaltered or you don't get
the licence, they said. But it wouldn't be true, he would say.
Never mind, they would reply, we quite understand. Well, I
don't, he would say.

As a solicitor, he was not much better. Law had seemed to
him an admirable profession and suitable to his logical mind.
Indeed, when in business he had more than once been told
that he should be a ruddy lawyer. But he found the distinc-
tion between knowledge that your client is in the wrong and
a firm belief to the same effect too nice a one.

'It's not for you to try the man,' said one of his partners.
'That's for the Judge. You may be wrong.'

'I dare say you're right,' he replied, 'but it requires a
person with a rather tougher conscience than mine to appear
for someone who I'm quite sure is in the wrong and who gives
every indication to me of being a thorough-paced liar, just
because he tells me, with an oily grin, that he is in the right
and can prove it by the evidence of some poisonous-looking
reptiles whom he calls his independent witnesses.'

So he gave up the law for teaching. This at first suited him
better. But there he found not his conscience, but his intelligence, outraged.

'It is perfectly ridiculous to try to cram all this into the
boys in one term,' he said to one headmaster.

'I know,' said the headmaster, 'but it can be done and it's necessary for the exams.'

'The exams should be changed, then. They'll forget most of it in the following term.'

'No doubt you're right,' said the headmaster with a sigh, 'and I don't pretend I haven't said and thought the same things as you. But it's no good. If you want to get on you must fall into line.'

'Permission, then, to fall out, please, sir,' said Mr Pudsey.

So he became a parson. And that really was his *métier*. It may be wondered why he had not become one from the start. The reason was quite simple. He had hoped that he could take into worldly affairs his strong beliefs and principles. He did not wish to be labelled a man of God by reason of his profession. He would have been very happy if, as a solicitor, he had been known as a man of God. Like all those who believe in God he did not think His presence was confined to a place of worship, and in the same way he hoped that, as an ordinary man wearing no dog-collar, he might have been able to carry on some ordinary calling without interference with his beliefs and principles. But it could not be done, and so, once ordained, he threw himself wholeheartedly into his new work. He loved it. He loved people, the good and the bad alike – often the bad the more, as they gave him more scope. He was never impatient; neither with hypocrites nor liars. But he tried to remove the veil, curtain, or brick wall by means of which some people keep themselves in ignorance of their faults. The process was sometimes a painful one for the patient, but he persevered, and only administered an anaesthetic in cases where it was essential.

It was, then, on this formidable character that Basil called in accordance with his appointment.

'I don't think we've met before,' said the parson.

'I have seen you about,' said Basil.

'Ah, then you are one of my parishioners?'

'I'm afraid we're not regular churchgoers.'

'Ah, then you have been sometimes?'

Basil began to realize quickly that, if some parsons lack intelligence, this one certainly didn't.

'I'm afraid not.'

'Total abstainers, eh?' said the parson. 'Not on principle, I hope.'

Basil decided to put up a fight. He enjoyed one, and it was a long time since the last.

'For lack of it, I fear.'

When you are really going to attack in argument you run with your opponent until the right moment occurs.

'And you'd like some help? I'm delighted.'

He looked at Basil's bald patch and greying hair.

'It's never too late, you know.'

'That's good news,' said Basil, still running with the hare.

'Now tell me,' said the parson, 'if you'll forgive an intimate question on such an early acquaintanceship, would you describe yourself as a thoroughly unprincipled man? Don't be alarmed at the nature of the question. We have several in our parish – very nice fellows, most of them. As a matter of fact, one of them is coming to tea this afternoon. No – I'm wrong, it's tomorrow. He comes out this afternoon.'

'Comes out?' said Basil. He knew quite well what was meant, but felt that he should ask.

'Prison, you know. Let me see, it was six months this time. I don't suppose you've ever been inside, but don't hesitate to say so if you have. We have no distinctions here.'

'No. I haven't – yet.'

'Good,' said the parson. 'Good. I wonder how many people could say today that they had never been to prison – and never deserved to. You couldn't, I suppose?'

'Mr Pudsey,' said Basil, who began to find running with

the hare somewhat irksome. 'I enjoy your frankness. But don't you ever find that people whom you've never met before and who, incidentally, have come to try to be of some service to you, object to being asked how many crimes they have committed?'

'Not how many,' replied the parson. 'Just whether any. I gather from the form of your questions that the answer in your case is, yes. Capital. I don't often have such frank admissions on a first meeting. We should get on well together. And now, I believe, you wanted to render some small service to the Church.'

'I didn't say small.'

'And what service from a puny, miserable mortal – I am not referring to you personally, you know, just to human beings in general – and what service from a mere man could be other than small? If you were burnt at the stake it would be a trifle to give your Creator in return for the manifold benefits He has given you.'

'It would not surprise me,' said Basil, 'if all sorts of comic things were done in this unusual household, but I don't imagine burning at the stake is one of them.'

'Indeed, no. I hope I am a kindly man. I feel well disposed towards all – even towards rich and thoughtless men who assume that wealth is a substitute for conscience. I try to help them, Mr . . . er Mr . . . ?'

'Have you forgotten my name so soon? It is Merridew.'

'Ah, yes – I shouldn't have forgotten it. Quite a public man really. If I remember rightly you had some most unfortunate publicity – I'm sure you found it most painful – over an enticement action you felt compelled to bring. Most distressing, I'm sure. And then my cousin at Tapworth Magna – he's the Vicar there – told me you stayed there for a short time. Your stamp collection hasn't turned up, I suppose? They do occasionally. It would be a long shot, but I'd ask one or two of my parishioners if they knew anything about it. Such strange coincidences do occur.'

This was quite wrong. The hare was apparently snapping at the hound and getting in several quite painful bites.

'Mr Pudsey,' said Basil, 'funnily enough, I, like you, am a patient man, and I have a great respect for your calling.'

'Not bred of familiarity, I gather.'

'But in point of fact I haven't come to discuss my own private failings with you. It occurred to me that there might be some Church undertaking especially in need of funds to which I could subscribe. You are right in thinking that I am a man of means. You will forgive me if I don't discuss with you the nature of my conscience. The position is this: I am a full member of your Church and I am willing to subscribe – quite substantially too – to any one or more of your funds, if you would like me to do so. If you do not, you have only to say so, and I will then ascertain whether your Bishop has any such funds which are in need of my assistance. I will at the same time inquire from him whether he approves of the clergy in his diocese going out of their way to insult their parishioners without the slightest provocation.'

The hound was nipping back.

'Capital,' said Mr Pudsey. 'Even for a patient man, you have shown great tolerance. Such men are rare. Most would have walked out. Offerings from such as you will most certainly be acceptable, and the larger the better. You are most kind. Incidentally, pray don't think I'm trying to divert your generosity from any of the Bishop's funds. And by all means report this conversation to him. He would be most interested to know that I had met you. We have discussed you several times.'

Basil thought quickly and decided not to ask for details of these discussions. Instead, he got out his cheque-book.

'A business man, I see,' said Mr Pudsey. 'I was one myself

once. We have a lot in common, I see – except, I hope, our bank balances. Now – would it be impertinent to inquire how much you propose to offer?'

'I had thought of £2,000.'

'That indeed is most generous. I accept it gladly. It will ease several burdens. Oh no, I was not referring to any light ones on your conscience. If you could go to £2,500, we could complete all the repairs we have in hand.'

Basil hesitated, but he made out the cheque for £2,500.

'That is indeed most kind,' said the parson. 'I hope now that we have met I shall have the pleasure of seeing you at one of our services. My sermons are quite short – and never directed at an individual. Do try and come, if you have the time – I realize, of course, that it must be difficult for such a successful man to find it. But think it over. So very glad to have met you, Mr Merridew. You see, I haven't forgotten the name this time.'

Basil left and was soon back at his flat, reporting the result of his visit.

'Not only did he call me all the names under the sun, but, having done so and after I'd threatened to report him to his Bishop, he pushed me up from £2,000 to £2,500. It was a lousy idea of yours, Nicholas. Perhaps I'd better go and see your flower-seller to make up.'

'I'll come with you,' said Elizabeth.

'Oh, well,' said Basil, 'perhaps it isn't worth it. But as for doing good being the answer – I feel like robbing an offertory box at the moment.'

'I don't know, old boy,' said Nicholas. 'I quite understand how you feel about it. I should have felt the same, but one swallow doesn't make a summer. I vote we have another try. After all, we're getting nowhere as it is. Bored to tears. The Vicar didn't bore you, anyway. You must admit that.'

'You're right there. At first, when he started on me, I

thought it would be rather fun. But I found I was getting considerably more than I was giving. He knows too much about us. D'you know, his cousin was the chap at Tapworth. That was a nasty one. Then he'd read all about the enticement case. I dare say he's added it all up. I thought I'd better pay and get out. I tell you, I cut a pretty poor figure. I bet he'll tell old Maitland Temperley all about it. He'll love it. However, you're quite right, Nicholas, really. We've got to try something – but no more vicars, thank you. How about advertising? We'd get a lot of crooks and cranks, but we might find something amusing.'

'Deserving people never ask.'

'I didn't say deserving. I said amusing. We've given £2,500 for deserving people. I'm sure that parson will see it's used properly. Actually, I've a sneaking respect for the man.'

'I don't think we ought to stress the wealth in any advertisement. Otherwise we'd want a staff like a pool promoter's to deal with the answers. Besides, mere requests for money can't be amusing. We want a job to do.'

'Agreed,' said Basil. 'Let's try to work out an advertisement.'

In consequence of many attempts, the following advertisement appeared in the daily Press a week later:

Bring your problems of difficulty to us. We have the means and ability to tackle most of them and if sufficiently interested we will do so at our own expense. No applications for money considered.

'Whose idea was this?' said Basil when they had the first batch of answers. 'We shall need a secretary to sort these out.'

'Elizabeth and I will choose one for you,' said Petula.

'How thoughtful of you, darling,' said Nicholas. 'Always ready to help. Talking of which, I don't see why you and Elizabeth shouldn't do them.'

They were right to expect crooks and cranks and, in addition, in spite of the warning in the advertisement, they had many requests for money.

'I was wondering, old boy,' said Nicholas, 'what it feels like to give away £2,000.'

'I've told you,' said Basil with some feeling.

'Ah, but it was different in your case. He tweaked your nose in the process.'

'I hope your flower girl didn't take the same or any similar liberty,' said Petula.

'No. I'm quite serious,' said Nicholas. 'I should like to see what it feels like. I shouldn't mind you trying it out, if you wanted to,' he added, turning to Petula.

'Why should I give away £2,000?' said Petula.

'It might make you happy,' said Elizabeth. 'At least that's what Nicholas thinks.'

'It might make someone else happy,' said Petula, 'but I don't see why it should make me happy.'

'Then why did you agree to our trying?'

'Oh, I agree to everything. That doesn't include flower girls,' she added quickly.

'I think I might enjoy giving away £2,000,' said Elizabeth, slowly, 'to some really godlike young man. I wonder what he'd do.'

'Take it.'

'Is that all?'

'That is all,' said Basil firmly.

'Oh,' said Elizabeth, 'I shouldn't get much fun out of that.'

'This all shows,' said Basil, 'that just giving away money – like that – isn't any good.'

'Except to a flower girl,' said Petula.

'That proves the rule,' said Nicholas.

'The rule is that there are no flower girls,' said Petula.

'What we want,' went on Basil, 'is a real job – something to tax our ingenuity.'

'Well,' said Nicholas, 'there ought to be something in that heap.'

There was. Among others there was a letter from Mr Buckram of Poppleton, acting for a number of residents in Tapworth Magna.

'My clients,' he wrote, 'do not wish to make the slightest insinuation against Mr Merridew, to whom they have already paid £10,000 damages, but in view of all the circumstances and in particular the information given them by Mr Pudsey, they feel that it is only through such an organization as yours that the matter can be fully investigated. They are not prepared to throw good money after bad, but if you could see your way to undertaking an inquiry into the relationship between Mr Merridew and Mr Drewe and the mysterious burglary – all of which our clients accept as being entirely genuine and straightforward – they will be deeply obliged.'

'That,' said Basil, 'could be worth at least another £10,000 except for the fact that they know too much and we don't want it. Shall we send them back their £10,000?'

'Why?' said Petula.

'Why not?' said Nicholas.

'You're always against me,' said Petula.

'Only when you're rude to my flower-sellers,' said Nicholas.

'We don't need the money, and just in case of accidents it might be the sensible thing to do. There'd never be a prosecution if they had their money back.'

'Mightn't it make people suspicious of the kitchen table?'

'They can be suspicious as long as they like. We're now a happy united family. So we were before Nicholas pinched Elizabeth.'

'I would never allow that kind of liberty,' said Elizabeth.

'Figuratively,' said Basil.

'Not there either,' said Elizabeth; 'least of all.'

'Never mind,' said Basil. 'They can't do a thing about that, but Tapworth is rather different. I suggest we let them have it back. Agreed?'

'All except the flower girl,' said Petula.

'She wasn't at Tapworth.'

'Agreed,' said Petula.

Some days later Mr Buckram, who received no reply to his answer to the advertisement, was surprised to receive the following letter.

Dear Sir, I have a grave objection to a wagging tongue, and while I lived at Tapworth Magna I considered that too many of them wagged. I hope that the loss of £10,000 in total was a sufficient lesson to the owners of those tongues and, as I never intended to do anything except teach them that lesson, I have – I will not say pleasure but some satisfaction, in sending you the sum of £10,000, together with interest at 5 per cent since payment to me. I hope that amid the cries of astonishment some of your clients will find time to say a good word for
Yours faithfully,
Basil Merridew

Mr Buckram read the letter through again to see that he had not made a mistake and then immediately informed General Purbrick. In consequence, a meeting of the persons concerned was convened by the General at his house.

'Well,' said the General when they were all assembled, 'what do we do? Do we take it?'

'Do we take it?' Judge Strachan almost yelled. 'Of course we do. Surely you haven't temporized with him. He may change his mind and stop the cheque.'

'Have no fear on that account,' put in Mr Buckram. 'I have already had it specially cleared. I thought there could be no harm in that. We can always send it back if you so decide.'

'Send it back?' said the Judge. 'Why on earth should we?'

'My dear Judge,' said the General, 'don't you remember our last interview with him? He made you perform like a monkey on a stick. I'm not sure that you didn't come off worst of all of us.'

'Well, then,' said the Judge, 'if I'm in favour of taking it, you all ought to be. If a burglar ties you up and spits at you and steals your purse, you wouldn't refuse to take it back just because he spat at you.'

'It's a point of view,' said the General. 'I personally don't want to touch the fellow's money. Look how he behaved at the cricket match.'

'It isn't his money,' said the Judge. 'He extracted it from us by threats.'

'No more than any other plaintiff does. What do you say, Mr Buckram?'

Mr Buckram was in a difficulty. On the legal aspect he agreed with the General, but he hardly felt it politic to disagree with the Judge, before whom he was to appear the next day.

'I think,' he said after a pause, 'that I understand both points of view. I will do whatever I'm instructed.'

'But you must have a mind, man,' said the General. 'What do you think? We'll instruct you later on. At the moment we're asking for your advice. That's what you're here for, isn't it?'

'Well, Sir Bragge,' said Mr Buckram rather unhappily, 'if it were my money . . .' He paused.

The General and the Judge looked hard at him. He did quite a lot of work for the General, and sometimes he did it before the Judge.

'Yes, if it were your money,' said the General and the Judge together.

Mr Buckram gulped and plunged. 'I should take it,' he said.

'You lawyers,' said the General. 'What about your pride, man?'

'It's easy for you to talk,' said the Judge. 'Rich men can afford to have pride. What do you say, Doctor?'

'If you ask me,' said the Doctor, 'the man's mad. He's a pathological case. In the normal way, I shouldn't take money from a lunatic, but as he's taken it off me first, I don't see why I shouldn't. Yes, I support you, George.'

'Well, Vicar,' said the General, 'you've been very quiet.'

'You forget. I don't really come into this. Nicholas insisted on paying my share. I wouldn't take it. So we compromised by giving it to the Church Restoration Fund.'

'But he's included it in the cheque.'

'Yes, of course, he would. He wouldn't know about Nicholas. Well, that had better go to the Restoration Fund too. I personally wouldn't touch a penny from the man.'

The Vicar recollected with some feeling his last two interviews with Basil. 'But I don't see why he shouldn't help the Church. No, on the whole I agree with the Judge.'

Eventually it was agreed by a large majority to accept the money.

'Very well, then,' said Mr Buckram. 'What shall I say in reply?'

'I acknowledge with thanks your cheque, which will be distributed among the parties entitled thereto,' said the Judge.

'Oh, no,' said the General. 'I'm entirely against taking the money, but you've outvoted me. So that's that. But if we are taking it we must take it graciously. Give the fellow his due, he needn't have sent it. We needn't take it, but if we do we should do it properly.'

As a result of some further discussion Basil eventually received the following letter:

Dear Sir, My Clients were, as you imagined, astonished to hear of your letter and enclosure. They are bound to say that they did not understand your behaviour at Tapworth Magna any more than they understand your present attitude. At the same time they recognize that you are plainly making a most generous gesture towards them, and while still puzzled at it they have instructed me to accept your cheque in the same spirit as that in which it is offered – whatever that may have been.

'Good,' said Basil. 'We can close that episode now. Now what about the expelled schoolboy? I must say it rather intrigues me.'

He was referring to another of the replies to their advertisement. It ran as follows:

In answer to your advertisement, we should like to consult you about a most painful matter which seems incapable of remedy. Our only son has been expelled from his preparatory school for cheating in an examination. We are quite sure that he is innocent, but apparently have no redress. His whole career will be ruined and our hearts broken. We note that you do not require financial assistance, but we should make it plain that we should be very pleased to pay anything in order to get this grave injustice put right.

'Let's see them,' said Basil.

'No harm,' said Nicholas.

So an appointment was arranged.

Mr and Mrs Wesley-Hart were the proud but unhappy parents of one son, Kenneth, who was just thirteen at the time of their appointment with Basil and Nicholas. Until his retirement from a successful drapery business, started in a small way by his father, Mr Wesley-Hart had been known as Hart, but Mrs Hart thought that the addition of Wesley might take people's minds off the drapery business. They sent their boy to a large and expensive preparatory school called 'The Summit'. They intended him to go to a well-known public school and thence to Oxford or Cambridge. After that the Bar and politics. It all sounded so good and

Mrs Wesley-Hart was never tired of telling her friends about young Kenneth's prospects. No business career for him. She had been delighted when her husband sold out lock, stock, and barrel. They were not wealthy, but they had ample means to carry out their plans for their boy and to ensure themselves a comfortable home. And now it was all finished. No public school would take a boy expelled for cheating, no university, no Inn of Court. It might be that the House of Commons did contain here and there a member whose past would not bear the closest scrutiny, but how awkward at an election.

'Weren't you expelled for cheating?'

'That was twenty years ago.'

'Have you improved since then?'

The hecklers would be able to have a high old time with him, they thought, as their imagination ran riot. But worse than that was the immediate future. He was just about to go to his public school. And now this. Where could he go? It was too dreadful. They had interviewed the Headmaster three times, they had employed a solicitor and they had been to counsel. Each time the answer was the same: 'I'm sorry, but it is quite hopeless.' Then they saw the strange advertisement. It could do no harm to try.

'Come in, Mr and Mrs Wesley-Hart,' said Basil.

'And this, I suppose, is your son?'

'Yes; this is Kenneth. How d'you do? It's kind of you to see us.'

'Your letter interested us. Please tell us all about it. I realize how strongly you feel, but try to explain about it as objectively as possible.'

'What does that mean?' said Mrs Wesley-Hart.

'Never mind,' said Basil. 'Just tell us the story.'

What had happened was this. Kenneth and another boy, Leader, had been sitting next to each other during the end-of-term examination. The practice at the school for that examination was for each paper to be marked by two masters independently. The average mark was awarded. After the examination the papers had been collected and Kenneth's paper had gone to Mr Scales and Leader's to Mr Twine. When they exchanged papers they chatted for a few minutes about them.

'Quite a good paper from Wesley-Hart,' said Mr Scales. 'A few silly mistakes, though.'

'It's a pity they so often spoil it like that. I've the same tale to tell. A good paper by Leader, but again some silly mistakes.' So spoke Mr Twine.

Much was the surprise of Mr Scales and Mr Twine – and it afforded some relief to the burden of correcting papers – to find that the mistakes of Kenneth and the boy Leader, some of which had the merit of considerable originality, were almost identical. At precisely the same moment – by coincidence, they were correcting the respective papers at the identical time – Mr Scales and Mr Twine let out a whistle.

'My goodness me,' said Mr Scales.

'Gracious goodness,' said Mr Twine.

Coincidence was out of the question. Putting down the other papers, Mr Twine sought out Mr Scales, and Mr Scales sought out Mr Twine. They almost collided in the corridor.

'Extraordinary,' said Mr Scales.

'Amazing,' said Mr Twine.

It was unnecessary to mention to what they were referring.

'They must have been sitting next to each other. Let's find the invigilator.'

They found him, and on referring to his records it appeared indeed that Kenneth had sat immediately on the right of Leader. Both masters at once sought out the Headmaster, Mr Bulmer Riddington.

'May we speak to you for a moment, Chief,' they asked.

'I am always available to my staff and pleased to be of such assistance as I can. I myself often find that it helps to discuss one's problems with someone older and of more experience. But, alas, that is now denied to me and I have to commune with myself.'

This was quite true, and some of the more daring boys used to climb underneath his study window so as to hear the good man communing with himself.

Mr Scales and Mr Twine explained the object of their visit.

'I shall investigate this myself at once,' said the Headmaster. 'I can't believe that any boy in my school would stoop so low. What a disgrace! But it cannot be.'

However, on looking at the papers, he saw plainly that it had been.

'Send both boys to me at once,' he said.

They came, the one with some trepidation, the other wondering what it was all about – but which was which? That was not written on either of their faces.

'Boys,' said the Headmaster, 'never since I became Headmaster of this school has such a thing happened. I assume you know what I am talking about.'

'No, sir,' they each said.

'One of you is a cheat.'

They remained silent.

'A cowardly, wicked thing to do. Such a boy may well end up in prison – if not worse.'

'Come now, which of you was it? Own up.'

'To what?' said Kenneth.

'To what?' said Leader, a fraction of a second behind.

'This is worse than I could possibly have expected. To cheat is bad enough – but to lie as well, and to your own Headmaster. This is beyond bearing. Come now, which of you was it?'

Both boys said nothing.

'Will neither of you speak? One's as bad as the other. Now out with it? Was it you, Wesley-Hart?'

'No, sir.'

'Then it was you, Leader.'

'No, sir. I didn't cheat.'

'Nor me neither,' said Kenneth lapsing into his early grammar under the strain.

'You mean "Nor I either,"' said Mr Riddington, and paused for a moment. That didn't sound right. But it must be. However, this was no time for grammar. Cheating. And at The Summit.

'I will ask you again. You two boys sat next to each other at the end-of-term examination. Your papers bear such resemblance that one must have copied from the other. Come now. Which was it?'

'Not me, sir,' said Leader.

'Not I, sir,' said Kenneth in a slightly superior voice.

'I will send for you again in half an hour and then I will ask you again. You both know well enough who it was. One of you is a very wicked boy, and the other is not helping me as much as he could. The one cheated. The other didn't. The one who didn't must know the other did. Speak up, boy, and tell me.'

They both spoke up.

'It was him, sir,' they said in chorus.

'Go away, boys, and come back in half an hour.'

As soon as the boys got outside the Headmaster's study, they turned and looked at each other.

'Dirty cheat,' they said.

Meanwhile, Mr Riddington was communing with himself. 'If it was Leader, it wasn't Wesley-Hart,' he said. 'If it was Wesley-Hart, it wasn't Leader. So far, so good. And now what?'

He frowned. He clasped his hands together. He could not

see what. He tried to think what the great Arnold would have done. Bulmer Riddington had been brought up to be a schoolmaster, and he imagined himself to be like one of the great headmasters. He tried, as he thought, to fashion himself on their lines, and Arnold was his idol. 'He would have seen it in the boy's face,' he went on. 'His eyes would have pierced the boy's soul.'

He looked in the glass to see what chance he would have. He was not entirely happy about what he saw.

Meanwhile, the two boys were having it out together.

'You know you did it,' said the one.

'You know it was you,' said the other.

'I'll fairly kill you,' said the one.

'Dead men can't cheat,' said the other.

So the half-hour passed with a duet for the boys and a solo for their Headmaster. At the end of it they knocked at his study and were told to come in. He looked at them with the most searching gaze he had practised. Nothing happened. They both looked blankly back.

'Now, boys,' he said, 'I'll give you one last chance. Which was it?'

They pointed to each other.

'I see it's useless to argue with you,' said Mr Riddington. 'I must use sterner methods.'

He had considered thrashing both boys until they both confessed, and imputing guilt to the one who confessed the sooner. But, on the whole, although this would have rid him of some nervous energy, it did not seem an entirely satisfactory solution. Although, however, he had rejected this method, both boys suddenly thought of it and looked extremely apprehensive, the innocent one in particular feeling a horrible sense of frustration. They were both wondering what form their protest should take to the awful suggestion when Mr Riddington went on.

'Now, listen,' he said. 'Listen very carefully. One of you may think that he is very clever, but he isn't as clever as he thinks. There are ways and means of finding out these things. It is only a matter of time and the truth will be clear and will shine as brightly as ever. It will take a day or two, maybe a week, but no more. Now – now – if the guilty boy confesses at once, his punishment will be great: he will be expelled forthwith, but that is all. But if he does not confess now and we have to prove his guilt by the various methods open to us, then before he is expelled he will be thrashed in front of the whole school – and he will receive such a thrashing as will make the legendary ones of old seem like a caress. Now, Leader,' and he turned suddenly and snapped at him. 'Was it you?'

'No,' said Leader, and with sudden inspiration added: 'I can prove it wasn't.'

'How? Show me? Why didn't you say so before?'

'I've only just thought of it, sir,' said Leader quite truthfully. 'But I'd rather not tell you in Wesley-Hart's presence. Otherwise he might get round it somehow.'

The Headmaster seized at the chance.

'Leave the room, Wesley-Hart,' he said. 'Remain outside – beyond earshot,' he added. He rang for a porter. It was as well to be certain. As soon as the porter had come and withdrawn with Kenneth, Mr Riddington turned, almost too eagerly, to the boy.

'The proof,' he said. 'What is it?'

'I haven't any,' began Leader.

'You abominable liar,' said Mr Riddington. 'You are obviously the cheat. Heaven has cursed you and shown me the light. You wicked boy. Now you shall see my promise come true. Now you shall . . .'

'Please wait a moment, sir,' said the boy, 'I hadn't finished.'

T-F

'What more is there to be said?'

'That's what I want to tell you, sir, if you'll let me.'

'Then speak, boy. But I warn you that if any more lies fall from your lips I will thrash you here and now as well. Oh – never did I think that this would happen to me. Well?'

'It's just this, sir. I know I didn't cheat. So I know that Wesley-Hart did. When I said I had proof, you thought I had. He's only a boy, sir, so he must think so too. You know, sir, something connected with the two papers. Now sir, you've given him a chance to get off with expulsion. It's worth his while to take it if he knows he's going to be found out. Well, sir, if you pretend, when he comes back, that I have given you the proof, ten to one he'll throw his hand in. Don't you see, sir? He knows he's guilty. You don't, but I do, and so does he.'

'You mean,' said Mr Riddington, who began to see some force in the argument, 'that I am to lie to one of my own boys?'

'Oh, no, sir. I wouldn't suggest that. But if you just give him the impression that I've said something to you fairly convincing – if you just turn to him when he comes in and say: "Well, Wesley-Hart"' – and here Leader gave a very creditable and somewhat courageous imitation of his Headmaster – 'If you just say that, he'll crumple up. If he doesn't at first, you enlarge on the public thrashing. He'll say to himself: "If I'm going to be thrown out, I might as well go in one piece."'

'Well, boy,' said Mr Riddington after a short pause, 'I can't pretend I like the idea particularly, but there can't be anything wrong in just saying, "Well, Wesley-Hart?" and seeing if it has any effect. But if it doesn't, boy – if it doesn't –'

'If it doesn't, sir, you'll be where you started. So you won't be any worse off.'

'That borders on the impertinent, boy. Hold your tongue. Now,' and he rang for the porter.

'Send in Wesley-Hart, please.'

As soon as Kenneth came in, Mr Riddington turned to him and said in his most awful voice, 'Well, Wesley-Hart?'

Kenneth remained silent.

'Well?' he repeated, and then, throwing discretion to the winds, he took the plunge. Taking out his watch, he said: 'My offer of a painless expulsion will remain open for ten seconds, Wesley-Hart.'

Kenneth thought hard. What could Leader have said?

'Five seconds are gone,' said Mr Riddington, feeling almost as nervous as Kenneth. If the boy didn't own up he'd be sunk.

'Four, three,' he went on – in rather slower time than his watch was showing. Just as he was wishing he had never listened to Leader's suggestion and wondering what on earth he could do to save his face, Kenneth capitulated.

'All right,' he said, 'I did it. It's a fair cop,' he added.

'Don't use that disgusting language to me, boy,' said the Headmaster, but there was relief in his voice as well as anger. It had been a great strain.

'I'm not in your ruddy school now,' said Kenneth, 'and I'll say what I something well like.'

Mr Riddington was genuinely appalled at the language.

'You have not yet been officially expelled,' he said, 'and I warn you that if you use any more of that language, I shall thrash you for that. Now go and pack your things while I telephone your father. Leader, you may go too. I'm glad your good name has been cleared. I may tell you both now that I never had the least doubt as to which of you it was. It was clear to me from the start, but I wanted the culprit to have a chance of owning up like a man. Now go, both of you.'

Mr and Mrs Wesley-Hart naturally did not know the

whole story, but they repeated all they did know to Basil and Nicholas.

'But you say he's innocent,' said Basil. 'Then why did he confess?'

'Tell the gentlemen, Kenneth.'

'It was like this,' said Kenneth. 'Old Blunderbuss, as we call him, is a pretty good fool, and he was in a spot when we both said we hadn't done it. He'd have tossed up in the end, so I only had a fifty-fifty chance of getting off. How could I show it wasn't me? I wasn't going to have a thrashing into the bargain – in front of the whole school too.'

'But what about this proof Leader said he had?'

'He hadn't any. It was just bluff if you ask me. I don't know what he told old Blunderbuss, but, as he did the cheating, he couldn't have proved that he didn't.'

'It seems a very funny thing to confess to something you haven't done,' said Nicholas.

'It isn't a very funny thing to be thrashed in front of the whole school. I know the old idiot. He's as pompous as they make 'em. He had to have a scalp, and if the penny came down wrong, it was me. Why should I risk it? I didn't much care for the school, anyway.'

'But what about the effect on your future?'

'I didn't think of my future. My thoughts were all behind, if you follow me.'

'Well,' said Mrs Wesley-Hart, 'what do you think of the case? Can you help us?'

'There shouldn't be much difficulty about that.'

Both parents looked surprised.

'D'you mean that?' they said.

'Oh, yes,' said Basil, 'I think we could straighten this one out for you. The question is, whether we should. But,' and he hesitated a moment, thinking, 'there isn't really much to choose between these two boys. What do you think, Nicholas?'

'I don't mind,' said Nicholas.

'I suppose,' said Basil, 'there's no question of his going back to the school. What you want is an unqualified apology and an offer to reinstate him.'

'The term's over and he would have left by now in any event.'

'Of course. Then you want an apology and a letter of explanation to his public school removing the slur from his name.'

'Exactly.'

'I suppose we may be assured that Kenneth won't start confessing any more. It would be inconvenient if he did so just after we'd got a withdrawal.'

'He won't confess again,' said his father, 'or I'll give him what his headmaster didn't. It won't be in public, but it'll hurt as much.'

'Father will have his little joke,' said Mrs Wesley-Hart nervously.

'That was not a joke,' said Mr Wesley-Hart, turning to Kenneth, 'and don't you forget it. I haven't slaved all my life to have you expelled. You're going to be a great man or I'll know the reason.'

'Now, tell me,' said Basil. 'Where can I find young Leader?'

They told him.

'How much longer has he at school?'

'A year.'

'Very well, then. Come back in a fortnight and I think we will have some news for you.'

The Wesley-Harts left, protesting their thanks.

'What made you take them on?' said Nicholas.

'What else has there been?' said Basil. 'We might get a

bit of amusement out of this. All the other nonsenses didn't come to anything. I've just got to have something to do, and this is the best of a bad bunch. As for the Wesley-Harts – son and all – I'd expel the lot if I had my way. But then I'd expel so many people – there'd soon only be the four of us left, and that would be a dreadful bore. Come on, now. This is quite simple. You take Petula and go and see young Leader. Now this is what you'll do.'

He explained everything in detail to Nicholas and then made his own plans for taking Elizabeth to The Summit. Their visit was timed to take place a few days after Nicholas and Petula had seen Leader. They had seen him near his home during the holidays, and the interview had been entirely satisfactory from everyone's point of view.

One afternoon Basil and Elizabeth arrived at The Summit. They were seen first by the porter.

'I wonder,' said Elizabeth with her sweetest smile, 'if we could see the Headmaster?'

'Have you an appointment?' asked the porter when he had got his breath back. He had never seen anyone like Elizabeth before. Immediately Elizabeth produced the little frown. 'Oh, dear,' she said. 'Is that absolutely essential?'

'I'll see what I can do, ma'am,' said the porter. He had made up his mind that, whatever the Headmaster said, he would see Elizabeth. He was not actually prepared to die or leave his wife for her, but almost anything else.

'You are very kind,' said Elizabeth, giving him five rounds rapid of her smile.

It was not Mr Riddington's habit to see parents without an appointment. He was a big man in his own view, and big men can only be seen by appointment. He was very strict about this, and the porter knew it. But he had been porter for a long time and he knew that The Summit would not be quite the same without him. His burly figure had become part of the place. Just as some young men who are new to alcohol feel suddenly uplifted under its influence and pre-pared to climb the Albert Memorial and crown it with a frying-pan or even less suitable object, so was the porter under the influence of Elizabeth. The death roll among dragons (or knights) would have been much greater if Elizabeth had lived in those days.

'There's a lady and a gent to see you, sir,' said the porter.

'But I have no appointment for this afternoon, Albert. You know the rules. Send them away. Who are they?'

'They've a boy to enter for next term, I think,' said Albert, drawing slightly on his imagination.

'Time enough when they have an appointment. Who do they think I am? Let them go to some lesser place where, no doubt, the headmaster will be delighted to see them without notice. Send them packing, Albert. Give them a syllabus if you like.'

'You'll have to see them,' said Albert doggedly.

'Have to? That's a strange word to use to me, Albert.'

'You've never seen a lady like her, sir. You'll just have to see her.'

'Albert, are you out of your mind? What on earth are you talking about?'

'She's beautiful, sir, she's like one of them goddesses – not the fat kind, I mean, sir. You'll just have to see her. You wouldn't thank me if I sent her away.'

Mr Riddington hesitated. He was a moral man and seldom allowed his eyes to travel across the road, however great the temptation. He had plenty of self-control in this respect, and it was beneath his dignity to act like ordinary men on the top of an omnibus whose heads swing backwards and forwards as every pretty face passes beneath them, rather like the heads of spectators at a game of tennis. But he was a man, and if one of the parents of a pupil of his was exceptionally good-looking, he saw no harm in paying her a little extra attention. He had never seen Albert like this before. It was difficult not to feel intrigued. Eventually he said:

'Don't be ridiculous, Albert. I'm not in the least interested in what the parents look like. But as it's for next term and they've taken the trouble to come here, I'll see them as a special favour. But make that plain to them, Albert. A special favour – a very special favour – as I happen to be disengaged.'

'Thank you, sir. Oh, thank you,' said Albert, and almost ran back to Basil and Elizabeth.

'I've fixed it, ma'am,' he said, and looked at Elizabeth for his reward. She gave it him in full measure, five rounds deliberate. If it was possible for a human being to dissolve, Albert would have done so in his ecstasy. After he had recovered sufficiently, he asked their name and led them to the Headmaster's study. Just before they reached the room, he managed to whisper to Basil: 'He don't usually see people without appointment, sir. So, to oblige me, sir, you might thank him rather special.'

'To oblige you?' said Elizabeth, who had heard. 'Of course,' and her smile nearly made Albert's legs collapse beneath him. They had quite a big job to do, anyway.

'Mr and Mrs Merridew,' announced Albert.

'Pray come in,' said Mr Riddington in his most dignified voice, 'and be seated.'

He shook hands with them, and he was bound to admit that Albert had not exaggerated when he spoke of Elizabeth. This was going to be a pleasant interview. He would invite them to tea.

'It is so very kind of you,' said Elizabeth, 'to see us without an appointment. We know how busy you must be.'

'Not at all, madam, not at all. I am only too pleased to see parents whenever I am free. I am delighted.' He looked at

Elizabeth for as long as he could. 'Delighted,' he repeated.

'I'm afraid we're not parents,' said Elizabeth.

Mr Riddington thought for a moment. This was one of the greatest compliments he had ever been paid. They were about to enter their child before birth. The M.C.C. wasn't in it.

'Quite,' he beamed, 'but, although it is advisable to enter boys well in advance, I don't think all that notice is necessary – and, of course, it might be a girl.'

Elizabeth gave him two rounds deliberate. 'I'm afraid we haven't come to enter a boy at all. Didn't the porter explain?' They had not told the porter the object of their visit. 'But, of course, he couldn't have. We never told him.'

Never mind, thought Mr Riddington; this is very pleasant. Pity I can't send the husband out to play with the boys. Stupid-looking sort of fellow. Can't think how she fell for him. Now, here, as Mrs Riddington, mistress of The Summit, she would make the school even more famous. But the fellow's quite young, bother it, he thought, and he looks in good health. Perhaps Smith Minor could persuade him to fall down the disused well. But, really, I mustn't think of such things. He pulled himself together just in time. He had nearly said his last thought out loud.

'And what, then, can I have the pleasure of doing for you, madam?'

'It's like this,' said Basil, taking up the running. 'We're interested in one of your boys.'

'Godparents, perhaps,' said Mr Riddington. 'I'm delighted. So many godparents disregard their responsibilities. And who is the dear boy, madam?' He turned again to Elizabeth. She rewarded him with one deliberate while Basil went on.

'As a matter of fact, he's just left.'

'Indeed? I shall be most interested to hear about him. I

always follow up our boys' careers with great interest. Do you know, madam, that we have produced three cabinet ministers and a field-marshal, not to mention poets, novelists, composers and others – but, tell me, how long ago did he leave?'

'He's only just left. I'm afraid it was under rather a cloud.'

'A cloud, madam?' He had got into the habit of addressing all his remarks to Elizabeth even when he was answering Basil.

'A cloud, madam?' he repeated. 'But – ' And then the awful thought occurred to him. They couldn't have come about young Wesley-Hart. He had already had three interviews with the parents and, at the last, he had been compelled to call the porter and ask him to show the lady and gentleman out. He had nearly had to add: 'Whether they like it or not.' This lovely creature couldn't surely have any connexion with that disgraceful episode. But who else could it be? No one but Kenneth Wesley-Hart had left his school under a cloud. Oh dear, oh dear, he thought, and I was going to ask them to tea. I should still like to do so, but I can't have that dreadful case gone into again. Elizabeth, realizing what was going on, gave him ten rounds rapid and five deliberate. She was a little dismayed to find that, although they all must have hit the target, it remained intact.

'You can't be referring to – ' he paused, hoping against hope.

'To young Wesley-Hart?' said Basil. 'Yes, I'm afraid so. We have the boy's interests very much at heart, and his parents'.'

Elizabeth was now firing steadily, but with too little effect. Mr Riddington stood up.

'I'm extremely sorry, but the case is closed. Quite closed. Finished. Done with. Over. There is nothing to be said on the subject.'

'I fully appreciate your feelings,' said Basil. 'It must have been most distressing for you.'

'It was a disgrace,' said Mr Riddington, 'and we are trying to forget it.'

'How well I understand,' said Elizabeth, firing now almost frantically.

'The truth is,' said Basil, 'that the boy's parents believe in his innocence, and nothing that anyone can say can shake them.'

'I'm sorry,' said Mr Riddington, 'but there's nothing more I can do about it. The boy has only himself to blame.'

'They are talking about bringing a law action to clear his name.'

'An action?' said Mr Riddington. 'I can't think what for. But they must do as they are advised.'

'It would be so unpleasant for the school, though, to have Court proceedings.'

'Most unpleasant, but I can't help that, I'm afraid. It will be more unpleasant for the parents. Such proceedings are costly, I gather.'

'They don't worry about that. They look upon it like the Archer-Shee case and don't mind what it costs them.'

'The Archer-Shee case? Oh, yes – you mean the case where a man called Rattigan appeared in some capacity. But there's nothing I can do. If they choose to make fools of themselves and ruin themselves into the bargain, that's not my fault.'

'One thing had occurred to me – and to my wife,' said Basil, inclining his head slightly towards Elizabeth, who was busy reloading. 'The Wesley-Harts rely upon us a great deal, and if we can satisfy them that there is nothing more to be done it may be that they'll take our advice.'

'But I gather you've already so advised them.'

'We have, but, of course, we've never seen the proof for ourselves. Now we've seen you and had your assurances on the subject, that should be a help.'

'Well, you have them.'

'I wonder if we could also just see the boy Leader? The Wesley-Harts have never seen him. Now, if we could report that we'd seen him and heard his denials and were satisfied that it was hopeless to do anything more, they might at last be persuaded by us.'

'But why should I do this? Why should the boy Leader be worried any more about it?'

'For the good of the school, Dr Riddington,' put in Elizabeth, coupling her remarks with intense rapid fire and giving him a doctorate to which he was not entitled.

'It would be horrible,' she went on, 'to have this lovely school made a headline in the newspapers. You can't stop people bringing law actions.'

'Think of the effect on your pupils,' added Basil. 'What work would they do while the case was in progress? They'd be reading the papers all the time – that includes the picture papers too.'

'Picture papers?' said Mr Riddington, with some horror.

'Yes, you can't stop the Press taking photographs, and they get in everywhere. Just imagine "The Hall at The Summit", "The Baths at The Summit", "Cricket in progress at The Summit", "The Laboratory at The Summit". By mistake it would probably be a picture of the lavatories, but you wouldn't be able to do anything about it. Then the Press would try to interview your boys. "What do you think of your Headmaster?" they'd ask. The best boys would describe you as you really are, but just think what some of the young rascals might say. The public would lap it up. It would be horrible and so undeserved.'

'I should think of you when I read about it,' said Elizabeth sympathetically, and firing (metaphorically) from the hip.

'D'you mean to say they could do all this by bringing a trumpery action of some kind which is bound to fail?'

'Not only could, but will, unless we can stop them. That's why we're here. It seemed such a shame,' said Basil.

'We hadn't met you then,' said Elizabeth, 'but now that we have, we feel even more strongly about it. Do let us help you,' she said imploringly, firing volley after volley.

The attack was in too great strength and Mr Riddington capitulated.

'Well,' he said, 'there can be no great harm in your seeing the boy. And, if that will finish it all, I shall be much indebted to you, madam.'

'How wise you are,' said Elizabeth, and relaxed. She was now only firing an occasional sniping shot, just to make him keep his head down.

Mr Riddington rang the bell and told the porter to bring Leader to him. The boy soon arrived.

'These are my friends.' At the word 'friends' Mr Riddington paused and looked for a second at Elizabeth to see if she confirmed the word. She did, and he went on: 'My friends, Mr and Mrs Merridew.'

Leader looked at them, but said nothing.

'Come along, my boy, where are your manners? Say how d'you do?'

Basil and Elizabeth shook hands with the boy, and then Mr Riddington continued:

'Now, my boy, I'm sorry to have to worry you again but, for reasons which don't really concern you, I want you to assure my friends that it was Wesley-Hart who cheated last term and not you.'

Leader remained silent.

'Come along, my boy, speak up,' said Mr Riddington. 'I

expect he's nervous,' he added. 'There's no need to be, my boy. There's nothing to worry about. Just say that to Mr and Mrs Merridew and then you may go.'

Leader still said nothing. Mr Riddington became a little irritated.

'Come along now. Do what you're told,' he said.

'I can't,' said Leader.

'Nonsense, boy. There's nothing to be ashamed of. You didn't give the boy away. On the contrary, in a misguided sense of loyalty, you stood up for him until I found out the truth. Now that that is known, there's no need whatever for you to behave like this. Come along, then, speak up.'

'I can't,' repeated Leader.

'You not only can, but you will,' said Mr Riddington, who did not like the lovely Elizabeth to see him almost defied by a small boy.

'You wouldn't have me lie to them, sir, would you?' said Leader.

'Of course not. I only want the truth. Repeat what you told me – that it wasn't you who cheated.'

'But it isn't true,' said Leader, hanging his head.

For a moment, Mr Riddington said nothing. Then, in almost a whisper, but very distinctly, he said: 'What did you say, boy?'

'It was I who cheated, sir.'

There was no doubt about it this time.

'You?' said Mr Riddington in loud and horrified tones.

'Yes, sir. I'm afraid so.'

'And yet you told me over and over again that it was not you, and you let me expel another boy in your place.'

'I'm very sorry, sir,' said Leader.

'Sorry, sir?' said Mr Riddington. 'Sorry. Before this matter is done with, you will be so sorry – But why have you not told me before?'

'I was frightened, sir.'

'Then why now?'

'My conscience, sir. That talk you gave us on playing the game, sir. It was more than I could bear. I was just going to tell you about it when you sent for me, sir.'

'Very well, Leader, you may go for the moment. I will see you afterwards. We shall have a long and painful interview. Go away now – you wicked, abominable boy.'

Leader left and the Headmaster remained speechless for a moment or two after he had gone. He paced up and down the floor. 'But what I can't understand is why the other boy admitted it – it doesn't make sense.'

'Ah, but it all makes sense now. Kenneth has always told his parents that he only confessed because he was sorry for the other boy. I expect you noticed when he was at school that he was a very generous boy – always helping other boys and giving things away.'

'I hadn't,' said Mr Riddington. 'Quite the contrary, but no matter. Appearances are sometimes deceptive.'

'They must be, Dr Riddington,' said Elizabeth. 'I spoke to Kenneth about it. "Didn't you think of your own parents?" I asked? "Aren't they as important as the other boy?" He broke down then, and that's really why we're here. At first he wouldn't allow us, but when I pointed out about his own people, he began to see that he was wrong.'

'This is a terrible situation,' said Mr Riddington. 'I don't know what to do. How could I tell which of them it was? What can I do?'

'Let us help you, dear Dr Riddington. We are your friends,' said Elizabeth. She was now mounted and leading the victorious charge. The battle was over.

Shortly after tea, Basil and Elizabeth left The Summit, taking with them an unqualified apology signed by the Headmaster and addressed 'To whom it may concern'. In it he absolved Kenneth from all blame except an excess of quixotism. He described him as a boy of sterling worth and lofty ideals who would be a credit to any school which was lucky enough to have him.

As soon as Basil and Elizabeth had left, Mr Riddington sent for Leader.

'And now,' he said, 'now, you miserable, wicked creature, what have you to say before I pass sentence upon you? You can expect no mercy – be sure of that, but I will listen to anything you have to say in extenuation of your terrible offence.'

'Please,' said Leader, 'what I said wasn't true.'

'I know, I know,' said Mr Riddington. 'I know it only too well. But why wasn't it true? Why did you lie to save your own miserable skin and to ruin the prospects of your innocent schoolfellow?'

'He wasn't innocent, sir. When I said it wasn't true, I meant that what I said just now wasn't true. It was Wesley-Hart who cheated, not I.'

'Heaven give me patience,' said Mr Riddington. 'What have you said?'

'I lied to you and the lady and gentleman, sir.'

'You lied to us?'

'Yes, sir.'

'Why, in Heaven's name?'

'I suddenly felt so sorry for Wesley-Hart, sir, and – and –' He broke off.

'Yes, and what else?'

'And the lady was so very beautiful, sir.'

'You abominable scoundrel, how am I to know when to believe you? First you say you didn't cheat, then you say you did, and now you say you didn't. How can I tell which is the correct version?'

'Wesley-Hart confessed, sir.'

'And are you aware, you' – he could not think of strong enough language which did not go beyond the proper bounds – 'are you aware that I have just signed a document acknowledging that Wesley-Hart did not cheat?'

'Well, that's all right, sir. That'll make it O.K. for him. No one else will know.'

'Well, boy, whatever else happens, you shall have the soundest thrashing you have ever known. Whether or not you cheated – and I don't know now who it was – you have admittedly lied to me. Either you did so when you said you cheated or when you said you didn't. There's no gainsaying that, is there?'

'It sounds logical, sir.'

'Logical, eh? Impertinent as well. We shall see if you feel either logical or impertinent in ten minutes' time.'

'I shouldn't punish me, if I were you, sir.'

'Oh – you wouldn't, wouldn't you? Well, you are not me – not I – not me – and I am not you, and I shall now deal with you as I think fit, not as you do.'

'I really shouldn't, sir, if I were you. You see, sir, if you say nothing about this, neither shall I – honour bright – if you'll forgive the expression – but, if you take it out of me, sir, I'll take it out of you, sir, with interest, and I'll prosecute you for assault as well. I will not willingly be thrashed by you. I can't prevent you, of course, but you'll look a bit funny in the Magistrates' Court when the doctor describes the bruises as due to unmerciful punishment (you didn't use the word, sir, but you meant it), and when I produce the letter you've just signed (Wesley-Hart and I are on quite good terms really and I could get hold of it quite easily) and show that you really thrashed me because you'd made such a mess of it all, sir, if you'll excuse my saying so – well, sir, bearing all that in mind, hadn't we better cry quits?'

It will be seen that Nicholas had not wasted his time with

young Leader. The only piece of bad luck was that the former was not able to see his pupil performing. He was doing it very creditably – he had an excellent memory – and Nicholas would have enjoyed it. Of course, the boy had been given £100 and promised a further £100 – which was a satisfactory thought for him in case everything did not go according to plan. He felt reasonably confident, however, that, if he did not get off altogether, his threat of prosecution would prevent his punishment from being too severe, and it would easily be worth £200.

Meantime, Mr Riddington had also been thinking. There was no doubt but that, wherever the truth lay, he had made an egregious ass of himself. He would hate that to become known in the school, let alone among the public. It was blackmail, and he did not relish the idea of being blackmailed by a small boy. But which was the lesser evil? If he gave the boy the beating he undoubtedly deserved, there was no doubt in his mind but that the boy would carry out his threat, and the law – ass that it was – might say he had been too severe. Indeed, he intended to be too severe. The idea of the Headmaster of The Summit being fined for assaulting a pupil was unthinkable. If he beat the boy at all he might still carry out his threat and, even if the case were dismissed, he would be held up as a laughing-stock over the cheating episode. It was a terrible dilemma, but he had to make a decision.

'Leader,' he said eventually, 'you are a very wicked boy and will probably end up in gaol. You may even be hanged. But, for the sake of the school, I am not going to have this matter made public if I can help it. I do not ask for your promise, because it is valueless, but you have spoken to me of logic and perhaps you can understand this. The only reason I am not now going to punish you is to avoid publicity. If I find that such publicity occurs – through whatever agency – I will give you the punishment you so richly deserve.

Fortunately, you are leaving within a year. If you had not been, I do not think I could have taken this course. Now do you understand me?'

'Perfectly, sir. I no speak. You no cane. Permission to go, sir?'

'Get out,' shouted Mr Riddington, and his voice could be heard far beyond his study walls.

It was tempting to Leader to break his promise. It was dreadful to have to keep the story of the interview locked up in his head. But like the good blackmailer he was, he realized that the Headmaster could be pushed too far. The fear which makes the victim pay is that of publicity. Once there is publicity, that fear is removed and the victim will turn round and attack. And, after all, he had made £200 and had had a most thrilling hour. So he contented himself with the thought that he would call on Nicholas and Petula and tell them all about it, and he kept his promise to Mr Riddington.

The Headmaster had a very unpleasant half-hour communing with himself. 'What else could I have done? I wish I knew who had cheated. I'd have sworn it was Wesley-Hart after he'd confessed, but this fellow Leader would be capable of cheating his comatose grandmother. Yet, if it was he, why did Wesley-Hart admit it? I doubt if Solomon could have solved this one. Oh dear, oh dear. He was right when he said I'd made a mess of things. But who wouldn't have? I wonder what Arnold would have done.' The Staff at The Summit found him exceptionally difficult for the next week or so.

Meanwhile, Mr and Mrs Wesley-Hart ('you needn't bring your son', Basil had written) called on Basil and Nicholas and were overjoyed to hear the result.

'How can we thank you properly?' said Mr Wesley-Hart.

'I wish I knew,' said Basil, 'but, unfortunately, I don't.'

'I fear,' said Nicholas, 'that virtue must be its own reward, if that is an appropriate phrase.'

Some time later, young Leader called on them to receive his £100 and to describe the interview with his Headmaster. When it was all over, Basil said:

'A few years ago we might have found considerable use for that young man. I wonder what he'll turn into.'

'A highly respectable bank clerk, I expect,' said Nicholas. 'Like bright sunshine first thing in the morning, he promises too early. When I was his age, I had all the makings of a highly respectable accountant. Fortunately, I outgrew it.'

'I don't know so much about "fortunately". You'd have a regular job with regular hours. You'd come home to Petula each evening.'

'He would,' put in Petula.

'Sometimes bringing her some flowers or a small present.'

'Let's make it a small present,' said Petula.

'You wouldn't have had to think how to spend your time. It would all have been done for you. Petula would have had several children and — ' Basil paused. 'Well, now,' he said eventually. 'I wonder why we've never thought of that before.'

It was not at all a prosperous little community which lived round Sutcliffe Bowling. They had neither cars nor horses and they had virtually no capital. The Vicar typified the place. He had a large, cold Vicarage which was gradually falling to pieces, a wife and five children and a tiny stipend on which to feed his family and educate his children. He certainly managed as well as was possible, but it was an up-hill job. Everyone round him was similarly short of money and everything else, and the local pastime was borrowing. It was a game at which one could not hold the championship for long. Indeed, to become champion meant almost immediately complete eclipse. As soon as it was known that, say,

Major Brain had qualified as the most successful borrower in the neighbourhood, no one would lend him anything. The game divided itself into two parts; the first part was to obtain the loan and the second to avoid giving it back. The Vicar never joined in this game, but he acted as a sort of unofficial umpire. He would be approached both by those who were trying to recover a loan and by those who were trying to borrow something. To the best of his ability and with complete impartiality, he advised his parishioners as to the best course to adopt. Major Brain had in fact been very successful at the first part of the game and was battling bravely with the second. He was besieged on all sides – now by Lady Brill for the return of her mowing machine (which he had broken and couldn't afford to have repaired), now by the artist Paddy Langbourne, who, in a moment of lunacy, had lent him seven-and-six, and now by the local jobbing gardener who had lent him some pliers, which he had lost. It soon became fairly clear to the Vicar that Major Brain was the reigning champion, with the inevitable consequence that he found his way round to the Vicarage for consolation. Curiously enough, no one ever tried to borrow from the Vicar, but each succeeding champion made his way to the Vicarage for moral sustenance.

'It's absurd,' said Major Brain. 'I could easily write to one of my brothers, but I hate to worry them.'

'That shows a nice family feeling,' said the Vicar. 'Let me see, how many brothers have you?'

'Only two. There's H. F. Brain, the miler, you know. He's nearly ninety. And then there's that old scapegoat, Willie. He's nearly eighty. Both doing very well at the moment, I should say.'

'What makes you think that?'

'I haven't heard from them for so long. Oh, well, there's nothing for it, I suppose, I shall have to pop my dress clothes.

Never wear them, anyway. Hope they haven't got the moth. D'you know, I can't even get half a pint on the slate. Half a pint. Now I ask you, Vicar. I've a good mind to clear out and wind up the whole shooting match. How can a man live on an Army pension?'

'But where could you go?'

'Anywhere, Vicar. Become a tramp, I suppose. I might manage to pick up a thing here and there, I suppose. But I can't get any work here. Why, dammit, Vicar – excuse me – I'd mow old Charley's lawn for a pint, but he says he can't afford it, and I've bust the mowing machine. It's a pretty pass, Vicar. My poor old father would turn in his grave, if he could see me. Haven't even the price of a cigarette.'

'Well,' said the Vicar, 'have one of mine.'

'Now, I haven't come round cadging, Vicar,' said the Major, quite truthfully, but at the same time availing himself of the welcome offer. Then he saw that it was his last.

'Oh, I can't,' he said. 'I haven't sunk as low as that.'

'Plenty more in the other room,' said the Vicar, easily reconciling the lie with his conscience.

To Sutcliffe Bowling there came one day four strangers, Basil, Elizabeth, Nicholas, and Petula. They took the big house which had been empty for some years and which even the local authority would not take, as there was no one to put there. They bought it, with fifty acres, and started to settle in.

'I don't suppose they'll stay any longer than the last people,' the Vicar said to his wife, 'but I'd better go and see them.' He was very pleasantly surprised with his visit. Never in his time had any people arrived at Sutcliffe Bowling who seemed so anxious to bring in more than they wanted to take out. And they appeared wealthy, too.

'You want a new village hall, Vicar,' said Basil. 'Could you get a licence?'

'I expect we could get a licence,' said the Vicar. 'But it takes more than a licence to put up a village hall.'

Six months later the affairs of Sutcliffe Bowling were in the process of transformation. The quartet had come there to start families, but they soon found that there was plenty of other interesting work to be done. The setting upon its feet of a half-moribund community quickly appealed to Basil and Nicholas as a job worth doing. It was fun to see such immediate results. Even Major Brain, who was now starting to spend more time in the big house than in his own, did not worry them. Indeed, they found it an interesting question to decide how to launch him again on the world. Finding that he was quite clever with his hands, they eventually set him up as a jobbing carpenter. He was delighted and soon became able to earn the price of a pint or (on a hot day) even a quart. The Vicarage itself started to take on a different air. Elizabeth went to see the Bishop and arranged for the house to be repaired without the Vicar knowing who was paying for it. Just as they had been amused in the past at the antics of the people who provided them with the means of livelihood, so now they enjoyed watching the little people round them being reborn as a result of their help.

One day the Vicar and Basil were chatting.

'It's such an attractive name – Sutcliffe Bowling,' Basil said.

'Yes, it is a pleasant name for a village – but I'm bound to admit that, until you four came here, there wasn't much else pleasant about it. It's horrible to watch people going downhill and to know that the help one is giving is wholly insufficient. You ought to be very happy people.'

'We are, Vicar,' said Basil. 'Very. In fact, we always have been. Even when things weren't so good with us, we always found ways and means of getting along.'

'If one may judge from your behaviour here, you have

certainly deserved your success. You must have led almost exemplary lives.'

'Well, we've managed to keep out of prison.'

'It must have been a close thing sometimes,' said the Vicar, smiling at his little joke.

'Sometimes,' said Basil, smiling too.

Some other Penguin fiction
is described on the
following pages

WHEN THE GREEN WOODS LAUGH

H. E. Bates

1975

'There!' Pop said ... 'There's the house. There's Gore Court for you. What about that, eh? Better than St Paul's, ain't it, better than St Paul's?'

Nevertheless Pop could bring himself to part with the noble pile of junk for a song – to the tune of £10,000 profit. And if Mr Jerebohm, the Piccadilly farmer, imagined the Kentish yokels were dim, he was at liberty to do so. But the up-stage city wives were not at liberty to bring charges of indecent assault against Pop. He showed them why ... in court.

In the last of the Larkin trilogy H. E. Bates makes the Dragon's Blood and the double scotches hit with no less impact than they did in *The Darling Buds of May*. For the full Larkin orchestra is back on the rural fiddle, and (with Angela Snow around) the Brigadier may be too old to ride but he's young enough to fall.

'Pa is as sexy, genial, generous, and boozy as ever. Ma is a worthy match for him in all these qualities' – *The Times*

Also available:

THE DARLING BUDS OF MAY · 1602
A BREATH OF FRENCH AIR · 1685

NOT FOR SALE IN THE U.S.A.

DON'T TELL ALFRED

Nancy Mitford

1976

'Miss Mitford at her wittiest and gayest and ... most audacious' – *Scotsman*

Cracks in the upper crust are almost Nancy Mitford's private literary domain. She scribbles moustaches on to the family portraits with the irresistible glee of an urchin.

Many of the characters in her latest novel need no introduction to the thousands of admirers of *The Pursuit of Love* and *Love in a Cold Climate*. The scene is Paris, where Alfred (the husband of Fanny, who is once again the narrator) has been posted as Ambassador. Nancy Mitford is on the top of her sparkling form as she describes the effect on Parisian society not only of such old favourites as Uncle Davey and the Bolter, but of a younger generation who will undoubtedly become equally well loved. We might mention particularly the exquisite Northey (Fanny's social secretary and latter-day Zuleika Dobson), Fanny's own children (problems, one and all), and – but no, there are too many. Read, and be enchanted in your turn.

'Delicious imbroglio' – *Daily Telegraph*

NOT FOR SALE IN THE U.S.A.

MY OEDIPUS COMPLEX

AND OTHER STORIES

Frank O'Connor

1956

W. B. Yeats once declared that 'O'Connor is doing for Ireland what Chekhov did for Russia'. A patriotic boast, perhaps, but it doesn't take an Irishman to recognize the unpredictable liveliness and observant sympathy in these eighteen short stories. Their insight into Irish character and life never slides into sentimentality. Ranging from a child's confident misconceptions about sex to Sam Higgins, the honest headmaster, driven to exasperation and near madness by his slick and cynical rival, they are written with a freshness and fluency that is indeed Irish, but their appeal is world-wide.

'Frank O'Connor has long been recognized as one of the great short-story writers of this century' – *Time and Tide*

'Nowhere will you get so vivid, humorous, and deeply understanding a picture of Ireland as in these tales. . . . Anyone can enjoy his stories. All start with a bang and carry one through breathless to the end' – *Daily Telegraph*

'A miraculous technique which universalizes the stories without impairing their local virtue' – Muriel Spark in the *Observer*

NOT FOR SALE IN THE U.S.A. OR CANADA

ON THE LOOSE

John Stroud

1974

Old enough to want to run away from a loveless home, but too young to know where to go, Royston Beedman is a small boy on the loose. Royston is the wretched result of an adoption gone wrong – gone wrong because his well-to-do 'parents' thought that bringing up a child consists in paying school fees and buying expensive presents. He cuts a tragi-comic figure as his rebellious jaunts force him to spend cold nights huddled in beach huts or railway trucks. Driven to petty crime, he becomes 'a social problem', as well-intentioned but over-worked officialdom does its best to take over where the home failed.

The same warmth and humour mark this story as *The Shorn Lamb*, in which John Stroud retailed the experiences of a Child Care Officer – experiences which allow the writer to inject a feeling of real life into his novels.

'Beautifully done . . . the stress and tension are kept up excitingly throughout' – *Sunday Times*

NOT FOR SALE IN THE U.S.A.

MY FRIEND JUDAS

Andrew Sinclair

1980

'I've seen every steady affair I know bust up round this time. Joes and totties loving each other the whole year through, and suddenly spitting in each other's eye this week. Pills taking every chance to tread on their best friend's faces. All so goddam neurotic. If May Week's meant to be a rest-period after Tripos, give me Piccadilly Circus at midday any old time.'

For Ben Birt, a self-confessed parasite, May Week marks the end of an era. He has finished his exams. His girl has finished with him. And as Ben mournfully looks forward to two years of National Service, and back over three years at Cambridge doing everything but set-work and sport, Andrew Sinclair, author of *The Breaking of Bumbo*, explodes once and for all the myths about all those hallowed seats of learning.

'Very clever indeed. . . . This portrait of *la vie de bohème universitaire* should raise squeals of outraged delight . . . all along the line from Belgravia to Budleigh Salterton' – Peter Green in the *Daily Telegraph*

'A brilliantly readable comedy with an edge of bitterness . . . showing a very talented young novelist in the act of extending his range' – J. D. Scott in the *Sunday Times*

HENRY CECIL

Henry Cecil does for the law what Richard Gordon has so success-fully done for the medical profession. Among his brilliantly funny novels, of which eight are now available in Penguins, are:

Brothers in Law · 1745

Introducing the immeasurably young and ignorant Roger Thursby, who has just been called to the bar.

Friends at Court · 1746

'Cecil better than ever' was P.G. Wodehouse's comment on this story of Roger Thursby, now on the point of taking silk.

Much in Evidence · 1747

The law courts tend to get completely out of hand in this 'further instalment of fun and frolic at Bar, Bench, and Solicitor's office' – *Spectator*

Sober as a Judge · 1748

Roger Thursby is now a judge, and an array of entertaining and sometimes lethal characters now beset his sober path.

Settled Out of Court · 1990

In the story of a financier convicted of murder on perjured evidence, the author 'continues to do superbly what everyone now knows he can do well' – *Sunday Times*

Daughters in Law · 1991

The hilarious experiences of twin sisters in the law make a novel which is as entertaining and readable as *Brothers in Law*.

Alibi for a Judge · 1992

The case of the judge who had pangs of conscience. 'Improbabilities so imperturbably and amusingly put can only be enjoyed' – *Solicitor's Journal*

Independent Witness

His latest novel. 'Mr Henry Cecil's comedies of criminal life are in-genious, sprightly, immensely amusing from page to page' – Julian Symons in the *Sunday Times*. *Independent Witness* is published by Michael Joseph Ltd, 26 Bloomsbury Street, London WC1.